Change With Me

Also From Kristen Proby

Bayou Magic:
Shadows
Spells
Serendipity

The Big Sky Series:
Charming Hannah
Kissing Jenna
Waiting for Willa
Enchanting Sebastian
Enticing Liam
Taunting Callum
Honor
Courage

Kristen Proby's Crossover Collection
Soaring With Fallon: A Big Sky Novel
by Kristen Proby
Wicked Force: A Wicked Horse Vegas/Big Sky Novella
by Sawyer Bennett
All Stars Fall: A Seaside Pictures/Big Sky Novella
by Rachel Van Dyken
Hold On: A Play On/Big Sky Novella
by Samantha Young
Worth Fighting For: A Warrior Fight Club/Big Sky Novella
by Laura Kaye
Crazy Imperfect Love: A Dirty Dicks/Big Sky Novella
by K.L. Grayson
Nothing Without You: A Forever Yours/Big Sky Novella
by Monica Murphy

The Fusion Series:
Listen To Me
Close To You
Blush For Me
The Beauty of Us
Savor You

No Reservations
Tempting Brooke
Wonder With Me

The Romancing Manhattan Series:
All the Way
All It Takes
After All

Change With Me

A With Me In Seattle Novella

By Kristen Proby

1001 DARK NIGHTS

PRESS

Change With Me
A With Me In Seattle Novella
By Kristen Proby

1001 Dark Nights
Copyright 2021 Kristen Proby
ISBN: 978-1-951812-72-0

Foreword: Copyright 2014 M. J. Rose

Published by 1001 Dark Nights Press, an imprint of Evil Eye Concepts,
Incorporated

Sign up for the 1001 Dark Nights Newsletter
and be entered to win a Tiffany Key necklace.

There's a contest every month!

Go to www.1001DarkNights.com to subscribe.

**As a bonus, all subscribers can download
FIVE FREE exclusive books!**

Dedication

This is for all the girls who ever thought they weren't special. You're amazing.

One Thousand and One Dark Nights

Once upon a time, in the future…

*I was a student fascinated with stories and learning.
I studied philosophy, poetry, history, the occult, and
the art and science of love and magic. I had a vast
library at my father's home and collected thousands
of volumes of fantastic tales.*

*I learned all about ancient races and bygone
times. About myths and legends and dreams of all
people through the millennium. And the more I read
the stronger my imagination grew until I discovered
that I was able to travel into the stories… to actually
become part of them.*

*I wish I could say that I listened to my teacher
and respected my gift, as I ought to have. If I had, I
would not be telling you this tale now.
But I was foolhardy and confused, showing off
with bravery.*

*One afternoon, curious about the myth of the
Arabian Nights, I traveled back to ancient Persia to
see for myself if it was true that every day Shahryar
(Persian: شهریار, "king") married a new virgin, and then
sent yesterday's wife to be beheaded. It was written
and I had read that by the time he met Scheherazade,
the vizier's daughter, he'd killed one thousand
women.*

*Something went wrong with my efforts. I arrived
in the midst of the story and somehow exchanged
places with Scheherazade – a phenomena that had
never occurred before and that still to this day, I
cannot explain.*

*Now I am trapped in that ancient past. I have
taken on Scheherazade's life and the only way I can
protect myself and stay alive is to do what she did to
protect herself and stay alive.*

*Every night the King calls for me and listens as I spin tales.
And when the evening ends and dawn breaks, I stop at a
point that leaves him breathless and yearning for more.
And so the King spares my life for one more day, so that
he might hear the rest of my dark tale.*

*As soon as I finish a story... I begin a new
one... like the one that you, dear reader, have before
you now.*

Prologue

~Zane~

"It's all lies." I scowl at my manager of more than twenty years as I sit across from the older man in my office. He looks tired. Frustrated.

And I can't blame him. I feel the same way.

"Listen, Zane. This isn't the first time in the past couple of years that you've had a scandal. I know being a celebrity is synonymous with—"

"Hell on Earth?" I finish for him, narrowing my eyes. I know what he's about to suggest, and it makes me damn angry.

"Maybe," he says with a nod. "But you're a good actor. And before now, the tabloid scandals blew over quickly. No big deal."

"Not this one."

He blows out a breath. "I think it might be a good idea to lie low for a while."

"That'll just tell the world that I'm guilty. And I'm *not*."

"Go on vacation, Zane. Take a few months off. Get the hell out of Los Angeles. You need it. I'll handle things here."

"I don't like the thought of tucking my tail and running, Hugh."

"You're not. We can make an official statement if you'd like."

I scrub my hand down my face. "Probably won't matter, but yeah. Let's do that. I'll go up to Seattle and hang with Rina for a couple of days."

"Months," Hugh says. "You'll go for months. You're exhausted. You're overworked. And you've been in the news too much lately."

"Okay. Fine. I'm gone. I don't have to be on set for seven months. I'll take six of those to let this all blow over. Make it fucking blow over, Hugh."

"That's my job." The other man nods then stands and leaves the office.

I take a moment to gaze around the space at the trophies and plaques. The photos. The glamorous life of an Oscar-winning actor.

Lonely. Superficial. *Fake.*

That's what this is. I've known it for years. But it's my life.

One that doesn't fulfill me at all.

Maybe six months away will be good for me.

I grab my cell and call my best friend, Sabrina Harrison Demarco. I haven't seen her since the holidays, which was more than eight months ago.

"Shit, time flies," I mutter as I listen to the ring in my ear.

"Hey," Rina says. "Whatcha doing?"

"I'm about to start making some arrangements. Looks like I'm coming to stay in Seattle for a while."

"Oh. Really? I can get the guest room ready. Ben's at the gym, but I'll let him know."

"I don't think you want me in your guest room for six months."

A long, heavy pause follows.

"What's going on, Zane?"

"I'll tell you all about it when I get there."

Chapter One

~Aubrey~

I'm so glad that I drove into Seattle first thing this morning and not late last night.

I made it as far as Portland yesterday. I thought about pushing through those last few hours to get into Seattle by around ten in the evening, but I didn't like the idea of finding my new rental in the dark.

Now, in the warm glow of the mid-morning sunshine, I'm *so* glad I decided to wait because the city is beautiful.

I open the lid of the pink box on the passenger seat and scowl when I see that I only have three donuts left.

Three out of a *dozen*.

"I guess there's a reason I have thighs the size of Colorado," I mutter and take a bite of a maple bar. "No regrets."

According to the GPS, I have three miles to go until I make it to my new condo. I like the tall buildings that rise against the clear blue sky. The hustle and bustle of traffic.

And when I turn onto the street where I'll be living, I grin.

Green.

So much green!

I've lived in Arizona my whole life. In heat. Brown and *heat*. Scoring this new teaching job in the Pacific Northwest is a dream come true.

I'm even excited for the rainy season.

I shimmy in my seat and narrow my eyes as I scan the building.

"Two-oh-three A," I mutter quietly and then clap when I see the numbers on my new building. "There you are."

The person I'm leasing from said there's even a water view from the master bedroom. I can't wait to sit with my coffee in the morning and enjoy it.

But first, I have to unload my stuff and get settled.

The landlord sent me the code to the front door so I don't have to hunt for a key. I grab my purse and the last couple of donuts and decide to go up and get the lay of the place before I unload my suitcases.

"Thank God I found a furnished condo," I mutter as I walk up the single flight of steps. I key in the code and push open the door, feeling myself sigh in happiness.

It's just so…*pretty*.

Exactly as described on the site and shown in the photos listed, the space is decorated in a modern rustic style with gleaming hardwoods, gorgeous leather furniture, and a faux fur rug.

The kitchen, done in all white with black accents, is just stunning.

"Good job, Aubs." I grin and pat my back. "If you had to move across the country with nothing but what you could fit in your car, *this* is the perfect place to end up."

There should be two bedrooms. I set the donuts and my bag on the kitchen island and then take off down a hallway. A smaller bedroom with two twin beds sits on one side with a little hall bath, and then I walk into the master bedroom that makes me dance a jig.

A big bed with white linens and blue pillows dominates the space. There's also a dresser and a chaise for sitting.

But the view captures my attention. Heck, it makes me *swoon*.

"Hell, yes."

"Who are you?"

My heart jumps, and my stomach jolts as I spin and see a man walk out of the master bath. He's tall. He's frowning.

And he looks familiar.

"The question is, who are *you*?" Why did I leave my purse—and my mace—in the kitchen?

"You're in my condo," he retorts.

"No, you're in *my* condo," I reply and cross my arms over my chest, trying to look mean. "This is two-oh-three A. Mine. If you're going to murder-death-kill me, I'm going to ask you to take today off and do it to someone else because I've had a long drive, and I need to get ready for my new job. Now, see yourself out."

Is that *me*, sounding all calm and collected?

I'm never this calm. Or collected.

Seattle is clearly good for me.

"I hate to burst your bubble," the stranger replies, "but I'm not leaving. I leased this place, and I'm moving in today."

"But." I frown. "*I* leased this place. And *I'm* moving in today."

I stomp out of the bedroom and head straight for the kitchen, opening my bag to retrieve my phone.

I also set my mace on the counter, just in case.

"I can show you the lease."

"Same," he replies. "Landlord fucked up."

I blink, open my mouth, then close it again.

"What's in here?" He opens my pink box and surveys the goods. "These cake donuts are my weakness."

Before my eyes, he grabs one and takes a big bite.

"So now you're stealing my house *and* my food?"

"I didn't steal anything," he says with a full mouth. "Well, except the donut."

"You're going to have to move," I inform him. "I already paid for the first month and the security deposit."

"I paid six months in advance," he says, swallows, and then smiles. Suddenly, I know exactly where I've seen him before.

This is Zane Cooper. The actor. The *celebrity*.

He must see the recognition in my eyes because his go ice-cold.

"I can't afford to find a new place," I inform him. "It took me a month to find this one. And it's perfect for me. It's less than six blocks from the school I'll be teaching at, so I can walk every day. And it's furnished. Plus, it's close to the water."

"Definitely perfect," he agrees.

"Oh my God, why are you *here*?" I demand and prop my hands on my hips. "You're a gazillionaire. You could literally go *anywhere*. Why do you want my condo?"

"I'm not a gazillionaire," he says and crosses his arms over his chest. "I'm more of a trazillionaire."

"Pretty sure that's the same thing. So, go build your own building and live in it."

"Nah." He picks a piece of donut out of his teeth and shakes his head slowly. "I don't think I will. I'll stay here."

I blink at him and start to feel helpless. My savings is in *this* place. I don't have enough left to rent anything else.

And I don't have time. I start work in just three days.

Part of me wants to cry, but I'll be damned if I let this hoity-toity movie star see me upset.

So, I do the only thing I can think of.

I prop my fist on the opposite hand in a challenge of rock, paper, scissors.

"What are you doing?" he asks, raising one sexy eyebrow.

"The adult thing," I reply primly. "Best out of three wins?"

He blinks twice, looks from my hands to my face and back again, then shrugs one muscular shoulder and assumes the position.

"Fine," he says. "I'm going to win—wait. What's your name?"

"Aubrey," I say and lick my lips. "Aubrey Stansfield. And you're Wyatt Earp."

His lips twitch into a half-smile. "I only played him on TV."

I chuckle and say, "Ready?"

"Go," he says, and we thump our fists three times.

I land on scissors.

He fists for rock.

Damn it.

"Let's go again," Zane says.

One. Two. Three.

I land on paper.

He chooses rock again.

I grin, and his blue eyes smile back.

There's a reason Zane Cooper is the hottest sex symbol in the world. Good God, I might combust just from standing next to him.

All the more reason to get him out of my house.

"Last one," I say. "Go."

One. Two. Three.

I land on paper again, assuming Zane only knows how to use rock.

But he forms scissors.

I breathe deeply and reach for my last damn donut.

"That's mine," he says, and I whirl on him.

"This is *mine*," I reply hotly. "I stood in a bloody line in Portland for it, just this morning. I drove all the way here from Arizona. I'm tired. I'm a little scared. And now I have *you* in *my* house, and you won't leave. Even better than that, you just stole it out from under me."

"I won it," he reminds me. "Fair and square. The donut, that is."

I stop and frown at him. "Huh?"

"I won the donut. In the rock-paper-scissors game."

"I was playing for the condo, Wyatt."

He barks out a laugh. "Not me. I want that donut."

I consider him, then the sugar bomb in my hand. Finally, I just break it in half and give him the bigger piece.

"That's as good as you'll get because I need this sugar," I inform him. "You're really not leaving, are you?"

He sighs, rubs his hand over his face, and then shakes his head. "No. Out of principle, I'm not. And neither are you."

"I'm not living here with you."

"There are two bedrooms," he reminds me, sounding perfectly reasonable. "You can take the guest room."

"Fuck that," I explode, having just hit the wall of my patience. "No way. I took this place because of that water view. Because I want to drink coffee and stare at it. And I'll damn well have it. If you don't like it, there's the door, Zane Cooper. Don't let it hit you on your gazillionaire ass on the way out."

"Trazillionaire." He watches me for a moment and then nods as if he's made some kind of big decision. "Okay, then. Fine. I'll take the smaller room, but I'm getting a new bed. Those twins are for children."

"Just push them together and make a king," I suggest and walk to the door.

"I'm not in an episode of *I Love Lucy*," he replies. "Wait. Maybe I am. This whole situation is ridiculous."

"You're the one choosing to stay," I remind him before closing the door behind me and marching down to my car.

I sit in the driver's seat and dial the landlord's number.

"Hello?"

"You made a big mistake," I say immediately. "I just got to the condo, and there's a man here who claims *he* rented it."

"I just realized the problem this morning," the landlord says. "Sorry. I have another place on the other side of the city. It's not furnished, though. And no views."

I growl in frustration. "No. I don't want that at all. I can't believe this."

"So, you're staying, then?"

"I guess. Since you screwed up so monumentally. And I expect my money back since Zane already paid in full for six months."

He sighs on the other end of the phone. *Yeah, I figured it out, you scammer.*

"I'll refund it," he says and hangs up the phone.

I let my forehead fall against the steering wheel.

"Well, I guess that's something. Maybe I'll start looking for another place."

There's a knock on my window, and I look up into Zane's stupidly handsome face.

"Leaving, after all?" he asks when I open the door.

"No. I was just having a minor nervous breakdown. I need to get my stuff."

I walk to the back of the car, open the hatch, and pull out my two suitcases and one large tote. Zane immediately picks up the storage container and pulls one of the suitcases behind him to the stairs.

He's strong. Those pieces aren't light, and he just climbs the stairs like it's nothing.

I'm struggling to get the last case halfway up when he returns, takes it from me, and hauls it up ahead of me.

He may be a pain in my ass, but he's a helpful one.

"Where's your stuff?" I ask when I find him setting my suitcase in the master bedroom.

"Being delivered tomorrow morning," he replies. "I just have an overnight bag for now. I have to make some calls."

He leaves, shuts himself in the smaller of the two rooms, and I hear his rich baritone as he speaks to someone on the phone.

I can't hear the words, only the tone.

And guilt starts to set in.

Maybe it's only fair that Zane has this room. He paid for the whole six months, and the landlord is returning my rent. Though, of course, I'll pay Zane half each month. Just because he's rich doesn't mean he should foot the bill.

Why is he here? Why would he rent this little condo when he could have a huge house on the water? Or a trendy loft downtown.

I guess it's none of my business. Except, it kind of is because he's in *my* home.

I set my toiletry bag on the bathroom sink and quickly unpack, hanging my clothes and tucking my unmentionables in the dresser. I bought some new rain jackets, rain boots, and sweaters because it's going to *rain* soon.

And I can't wait.

Then, I take a deep breath and stand in front of the mirror, staring at myself.

Mousy brown hair and eyes.

Frumpy figure. I have curves where I shouldn't and no boobs to speak of. I've never seen a flatter ass.

And when I take out my contacts, I'll be in Coke-bottle glasses because I'm as blind as can be.

I'm just…plain. Invisible. Have been all my life. I don't have many friends, and I'm not one that co-workers invite to be a part of their wine tastings and book clubs.

And that's okay.

I don't mind being alone.

In fact, I prefer it.

But now, I have a roommate. And not just any roommate. The most famous man on the damn planet.

"How is this my life?" I ask the reflection. "And what am I going to do about it?"

I can't do much until I get that refund check, so I shrug, retrieve a notebook and pen from my office bag, and start making a grocery list.

I need to *not* worry about Zane and start focusing on everything I need to do before I start work in just a few days.

* * * *

"These steps are going to be the death of me," I mutter as I muscle six grocery bags through the door.

Zane hops up off the couch and hurries over, frowning down at me.

"Why did you carry them all at once?"

"Because I only want to do those stairs one time," I reply and sigh in gratitude when he relieves me of the bags and sets them on the island as if they weigh nothing at all. "And who goes back to the car for multiple trips? I'm no quitter, Zane."

He smirks and starts rifling through my grocery sacks, so I slap his hands away.

"Get your own food, dude."

"Why can't we share?"

I scowl at him. "Because I bought this stuff. It's what I like—my snacks, my meals. This whole roommate thing doesn't include sustenance."

"I'm not a great cook," he says, thinking it over. "I hired a chef to come in. If you want, I'll just tell her to make enough for two. Easy."

I blink at him, surprised. "Why would you do that?"

"Because she's coming anyway," he says. "I'm pretty sure it's no trouble for her to add enough for you, as well. It's no biggie."

"But you don't have to do that."

"Well, you might not like the food," he says and pulls out a box of macaroni and cheese. "She won't be making this."

"*I'll* be making that," I reply and yank the blue box from his grasp. "Do you have a problem with mac and cheese?"

"Yeah. It'll kill you. Do you know how many chemicals are in that? There's no real cheese in there."

"Stop judging my food." I start unloading the groceries into the pantry. "It's my emergency food anyway. I don't usually eat mac and cheese all that often."

"What kind of emergency?" he asks and leans his shoulder on the doorjamb, watching me organize the groceries alphabetically.

"You know, a bad-day emergency. This is comfort food, and I have to have it on hand. Just in case."

"In case of a bad day."

I nod and brush past him to get another bag.

In the process, I feel his heat and realize how short I am next to him.

My nipples pucker, making me scowl.

"Don't you have comfort foods?"

"Whiskey."

I raise an eyebrow. "I guess that counts. I didn't buy any."

He laughs, and then his eyes narrow on the bag of nacho cheese tortilla chips in my hands.

"Now those, I like."

"These?" I hold up the red bag. "Do you know how many chemicals are in this? There's no real cheese in here. It'll kill you."

"Gimme."

"No way. Mine."

He grabs for them, but I evade, hurrying around the island.

Just when I think I'm free, Zane catches me, wraps his arms around me from behind, and snatches the bag out of my grasp.

"You're a thief."

"Don't worry." His mouth is close to my ear, his voice smooth as silk. "I'll share."

Chapter Two

~Zane~

"Wait." Rina holds up her hand partway through my story and scowls at me from across the table. Because it's my first night in town, she invited me over to have dinner with her and Ben. "You're telling me that the landlord messed up and rented the place to both of you? And you're still living there?"

"It's only been a few hours," I remind her. "But, yes. I'm staying."

As long as the damn bed is delivered tomorrow. I'm not spending more than one night in a twin.

"Why?" She sets her fork down, already loaded with shrimp, and scowls at me. "You could go anywhere. You could come *here*."

Now she sounds like Aubrey.

"Why should I be the one to leave?" I demand, pointing my fork at myself. "I paid for the place. I *like* the place. It's convenient."

"It's just a little condo," Rina reminds me, and I look to Ben for help. He just shakes his head and shovels more food into his mouth as if to say: "*I'm not getting in the middle of this.*"

"It's not fancy at all," she adds.

"I don't always need fancy."

She gives me an have-you-met-you look.

"Okay, I like nice things. But this place is new and nicely decorated. Sure, it's not my house in Beverly Hills, but it's fine. And it's a ten-minute walk over here. I can get to the gym quickly. I know the area. There were no houses for lease nearby—which is weird, but true."

"Speaking of the gym," Ben says, changing the subject. "You should come with me after dinner. There's going to be some sparring in the ring. Hunter Meyers is in town, and I think Nate'll even be there, which doesn't happen often these days."

I nod, chewing my shrimp. "I'll go. How's Hunter doing after that head injury a while ago?"

Hunter's a famous mixed martial arts fighter based out of the Seattle area, who goes to Ben's gym. He was attacked about a year ago and was in the hospital for a while.

"He's doing a lot better. He'll never come out of retirement, but he seems to be content with family life on the island."

"So, you're both just going to abandon me and go to the gym?" Rina sniffs. "Maybe I'll go with you."

"No." Ben leans over and kisses her cheek. "It's a guy thing."

"That's sexist," she says.

"No, that's your husband saying he doesn't want to kill anyone for checking out his wife tonight." I wink at her and see the truth of my statement in Ben's eyes. "Besides, you have girls' nights with your friends. We don't claim *that* to be sexist."

"You can come to the next one."

I scowl. "I'd rather poke my eyes out than be submerged in that much estrogen."

Rina laughs and starts clearing the dinner table. "Fair enough. Okay, tell me about this new roommate of yours. What's her name?"

"Aubrey." I like the way it falls off my tongue. "I'd say she's in her mid-twenties. She's a teacher, and she has a backbone."

"What did you do to her?" Rina's eyes narrow.

"Nothing she couldn't handle." I laugh when she just cocks an eyebrow. "It's not like I debased her or something. We had words about the condo, and I might have stolen her donuts. And some chips."

"What's up with you and food?" Ben asks.

"You didn't see the donuts."

"Fair enough."

"Is she pretty?" Rina asks, pressing for more information.

I take a deep breath and think about the young woman I met this morning.

"She has the girl-next-door thing going on."

"So, not your type," Rina says. "At least this will be a platonic situation."

"Wait." I hold up a hand. "What does that mean? How do you know she's not my type?"

"Oh, come on, Zane. If she's the girl next door, she's invisible to you. You go for the starlet types. Long and lean with blonde hair and fake boobs."

"I think I should take offense to that."

"Added to that," she continues, ignoring me, "they don't usually have much going on in their brains."

"That's not a terribly complimentary thing to say about the women I've dated."

She shrugs and clears my empty plate. "The truth isn't always complimentary. Besides, starting something with this girl—which you won't do—wouldn't be a smart move."

Now I'm getting offended. "Why not? According to *GQ*, I'm highly sought after."

Ben snorts.

Rina rolls her eyes.

"I am!"

"She's a teacher in Seattle, Zane. You're a megastar in LA. Those two things don't really mesh well. Also, she's not like the other girls. She won't move on to the next hot actor and talk trash about you to the tabloids."

Maybe that's one of the reasons I seem to be attracted to her.

Because she's different.

I like her. She's smart and cute in an understated way.

But I barely know her. And I have no intention of dating her.

Even if she *is* intriguing and has the prettiest lips I've ever seen on a woman—natural or otherwise.

"Hello?" Rina waves her hand in front of my face.

"Sorry, what?"

"I just asked what you plan on doing for the next six months. It's not like you to just sit around. You're a workaholic."

"The thought of sitting on the couch for months on end is not appealing," I admit. "But I have a meeting with Luke Williams tomorrow at his downtown office. He has some projects in the works. I thought about trying my hand at directing."

"Really?" She raises a brow. "That's new."

"A different challenge might be fun. Maybe *not* being in the spotlight for once would be a nice change, too."

"Who are you and what have you done with my best friend?"

I laugh and shake my head at her. "We all grow and change, Rina. You know that better than anyone. I'll keep you posted on the meeting."

"See that you do."

"Let's head out," Ben says after checking his phone. "The other guys should be there by now."

"It looks like things are going well with you guys," I say when we're in Ben's car, headed to the heart of the city where Sound Fitness is located.

"We're great," he says. "She's the best thing that ever happened to me."

The fact that it's spoken so matter-of-factly tells me that it's the truth.

"Damn right," I say. "Her life's been turned upside down since she met you. She seems to be taking it all in stride."

"She hasn't said otherwise," he agrees. "She wrapped on the movie last month. Said you came to the set a few times."

I nod. Rina was in LA for a couple of months, filming a movie for Luke Williams' production company. The second in three years. I don't think she would have come out of retirement for anyone but Luke.

"She's damn good," I reply. "Always has been. I'm glad she returned to acting. More than that, I'm glad to see her so happy with you. With her life here. When she was in LA working, she enjoyed it, but she missed you like crazy."

His smile is lazy and satisfied.

As it should be.

"Like I said, she's the best thing that ever happened to me."

He pulls into the parking lot in front of his gym then unlocks the glass doors for us because it's not open to the public tonight.

Classic rock pounds through the speakers, Aerosmith's *Dream On*, and several men stand around the ring, all dressed in workout gear. Some are getting their hands taped, others are just there to watch.

"I had to tell my wife it was against the law for her to come tonight." A man I recognize as one of the gym's trainers grins at Ben as he offers his fist for a bump. "She's a Hunter fan. But when she hears that Zane was here, too, well…she might divorce me."

"Zane, this is Greg." I nod at the trainer.

"Here's hoping you're not single come morning."

Greg laughs.

Ben introduces me to the rest of the men. I recognize almost all of them from the gym.

And, of course, I know Hunter. He and I have moved in the same circles for years. He may be famous for sports, but celebrity is celebrity.

"How long are you in town for?" Nate McKenna asks as he moves up next to me. His long, dark hair is tied back, and his hands are taped.

"A few months, actually," I reply. "How's the family?"

"The best there is." His smile is sharp and satisfied. "And doing well, thanks."

"I take it you're sparring this evening?"

"Yeah, but I have to go easy on Hunter over there because he has a soft head."

"Fuck you," Hunter tosses back with a good-natured grin. "You give as good as you want, McKenna. It's been too long since I sent someone to the hospital."

Nate simply raises a brow and climbs into the ring.

An older gentleman I don't recognize stands to the side, helping someone with their headgear.

"Go knock him cold, son," he yells out without even looking up.

"That's Rich," Ben says, nodding to the older man. "Nate's dad. He's the guy I bought this place from several years ago."

"Ah, I see the resemblance now."

The two men in the ring circle one another, each sizing the other up. And then it's on. Kicks and jabs. Lots of smack talk thrown.

"You're losing it, old man," Hunter says and sweeps his leg, taking Nate off his feet and sending him onto his back.

But Nate regains his footing quickly and gives it right back.

They go three sweaty, rough rounds. At one point, Hunter lands and hits his head, and everyone stops breathing until he stands and gives the nod that he's okay.

"Does he have a death wish?" I ask Ben.

"It's in his blood," Rich says. I didn't even notice that he'd sidled up next to me. "He needs to fight like he needs to breathe. Have you ever loved something that much?"

I blink in surprise and watch the two men as they climb down from the ring.

Do I love acting that much? Where, even if it could kill me, I'd do it anyway?

I don't think so.

I'm thirty, and I don't have that kind of passion for anything.

"If your wife finds out that you fought tonight," Greg informs

Hunter, "she'll have your head."

"She knows," Hunter says. "I don't keep secrets from her. Besides, I knew that Nate was getting soft. Figured he couldn't do much damage."

"Julianne asked me not to kill you tonight," Nate says mildly. "I usually do as my wife asks."

I laugh at the trash talk and enjoy several hours with the guys.

It's late when Ben finally drops me off at the condo. When I walk through the front door, I see that Aubrey left the light on over the stove and a note on the kitchen island.

Z-

Your bed was delivered. They even made it for you. Fancy.

-A

I grin and read it twice.

Fancy.

Is that how everyone sees me? Sure, I like the finer things in life. And I've worked my ass off since I was a toddler in a cutthroat industry to be able to afford such things.

Nothing was handed to me.

And even if it *was* handed to me, so what?

"And why in the hell is this suddenly bothering me?" I turn off the kitchen light and head into my bedroom. Sure enough, the space has a bigger bed. It makes the room feel even smaller, but I don't care.

I only plan to be here to sleep.

I do wish I had the balcony with the view, though. I would sit out there tonight and breathe in the salty air. Think about things.

"Probably overthink," I mutter as I shed my clothes and leave the bedroom for the hall bath. I need a hot shower and a good night's sleep.

The place might be small, but even the guest bathroom is a decent size with a big, walk-in shower. The hot water feels damn good.

When I'm finished, I dry off and sling the towel low over my hips, then grab another for my hair.

I step out of the bathroom and come face to face with Aubrey.

Her brown eyes go wide and travel the length of me, pausing at my hips.

"Sorry, I was just—I was hungry." She swallows hard. She's adorable in an oversized college sweatshirt that covers her to her thighs. I wonder what she's wearing under there. "Sorry."

"For what? You live here." I wink and turn my back on her, then glance over my shoulder and find her staring at my ass. "What are you going to eat?"

"Huh?" She blinks and looks up at my face. "Oh. Uh, I don't know."

"I'll just pull on some pants and meet you in the kitchen."

"Oh, you don't have—"

But I shut my door, cutting her off. Rina's right. She's not my type. She's not tall and lean. She doesn't have heavy-lidded eyes that almost *dare* me to touch her.

There's not a vixen-like bone in her body.

But, damn it, there's just *something* about her that I like. And I'd much rather hang out with her in the kitchen than brood by myself in my bedroom.

I pull on some sweats, forgo a shirt, and saunter into the kitchen where Aubrey's sitting at the island, scooping up some ice cream.

"Want some?" she asks. "It's chocolate."

"Sure."

When both bowls are ready, she slides one to me, then digs into hers.

"Did you have a nice evening?" she asks.

"Yeah. I was at a gym downtown, watching a sparring fight. I know the owner."

She nods, taking another bite of ice cream.

"What about you?" I ask her.

"I wrote up some lesson plans for my first week at school, organized supplies. Listened to some podcasts."

"What kind of podcasts?"

"Serial killers." Her cheeks redden at the admission. I can't help but wonder what else I could do to make her blush like that. "I like to hear about serial killers."

"I played Bundy once," I say and take a bite. The ice cream is damn good.

"Oh, that's right. What kind of research did you do for that?"

"I spoke with the original investigators. People who knew him. I read a lot, watched documentaries. I studied for six months before we started filming."

"Wow." Her eyes are wide as she listens. She's truly *listening*. She's not starstruck. She doesn't babble. And she's definitely not just humoring me.

She treats me like a...normal person.

Maybe that's what I'm attracted to the most.

"Does it mentally put you in a dark place to play characters like that? By the way, if I'm too nosy, please say so. I just know that sometimes, even after only listening about stuff like that, it can put me in kind of a dark mood. I can only imagine that after being in that headspace for several months, it could really mess with you."

"You're not bothering me," I reply truthfully. "And, yeah, it was dark. I can't speak for all actors, but a lot of us learned some valuable lessons from Heath Ledger's experience after portraying a *very* dark Joker in *Batman*."

"He died from suicide," she says softly, her eyes sad at the thought of it.

"He didn't," I inform her. "It was an accidental overdose. But from what I understand, his role in the movie didn't help things. If you're good at your job, you *become* the character. So, if I'm playing something dark, I only let myself stay in character while we're filming. Then I go out to dinner with the crew, have some fun. Laugh. You can't dwell there."

"Fascinating," she says and licks her spoon.

Her little pink tongue has my cock tightening.

"How long have you been a teacher?" I need to keep my thoughts off her tongue.

"A couple of years," she says. "I teach first graders. I love the little ones who aren't jaded yet. They're eager to learn. Sometimes, they can be hard to wrangle, but I enjoy them."

"And you moved here from Arizona?"

She nods. "Yeah. I was sick of the heat. My granddad passed away a few months ago, and he was the only family I had. So, I applied for jobs out of Arizona and landed this. I'm excited."

I have questions. Why doesn't she have other family? Is she alone? No friends?

But it's none of my business, and she's yawning.

"I guess I'm finally tired," she says with a little laugh. "New places are always hard for me at first. But I think I'll sleep good now."

"Good."

"'Night." She sets her bowl in the sink, gives me a little wave, and disappears into her bedroom.

At least one of us will sleep well tonight.

Chapter Three

~Aubrey~

This is what I wanted.

I breathe in the early morning air and savor a sip of my black coffee as I watch the water from my little perch on the balcony.

It's cool this morning, so I bundled up in my favorite sweatshirt and leggings and brought out a throw blanket, as well. I'm used to the dry Arizona heat, and this is anything but that.

It's completely glorious. I'm convinced that with time, I'll become accustomed to the cooler, damp air.

When I woke this morning, I stretched in bed and then remembered everything that happened yesterday. My drive to Seattle, meeting Zane Cooper, and all of the banter that took place with him. He's smart. I don't know why that surprised me, really. I guess I just didn't expect it.

Even more shocking to me is…I *like* him. Last night, over chocolate ice cream, it was fascinating to listen to him talk about his work. I could tell by the way his eyes lit up that he loves it. He's proud of it.

And he should be.

I mean, he's arguably the most famous man on the planet.

How I ended up living with him, I have absolutely no idea. It's the oddest twist of fate. Like the universe laughing at me.

Zane Cooper is living twenty feet from me, and I have no clue how to handle the situation. Most people I know would try to seduce him.

I snort at the thought and drink my coffee, watching a man walk his poodle down the sidewalk.

Yeah, I'm not exactly the seduction type. Zane would laugh in my face.

Not that I wouldn't *want* to. I may be plain, but I'm a red-blooded woman and am as attracted to the hot actor as anyone else. I've seen him mostly naked on the big screen, and it was a lovely sight.

Last night, I saw him mostly naked in *person*. And let me just say, that'll do things to a girl.

The sliding door behind me eases open, startling me.

"Sorry," Zane says. "I was just going to grab some breakfast and wondered if you want something. I'm headed to a deli not far from here. They have great breakfast burritos."

"Sure. I'll have whatever you're having."

He nods. "I'll be right back."

So, he's hot, rich, *and* thoughtful?

It's a shame I'm not his type. Because having someone like Zane around all the time wouldn't be a hardship.

Right now, I'm just grateful that things are going well. If this condo had to be double-booked, at least I'm not living with a big jerk. Besides, I'll only really be here in the evenings. I work long days.

The neighborhood slowly comes to life as the sun rises higher in the sky. There's more dog walking, some runners, even a cyclist or two.

I've just finished my last sip of coffee when Zane pushes open the door once more and passes me a brown paper bag.

"Here you go."

"Thanks."

He starts to leave, but I gesture to the seat next to me.

"You can join me, if you want."

"I don't want to butt into your private space."

"It's a balcony, not my bed." I gesture for him to sit again and pull the burrito out of the bag. "Holy crap, this is a monster. I'll be eating it for days."

"It's worth it," he says with a wink and takes a big bite of his burrito.

We sit in silence, eating our breakfast and watching the neighborhood below. Zane wads up his empty wrapper and tosses it into the bag.

I fold the paper around the second half of my burrito and set it aside.

"I'm so full." I pat my belly and sigh in happiness. "I wish I could go back to sleep, but I can't. I have a full day of getting ready for school. What are you up to today? Not that you have to tell me, I'm just making conversation."

"I know." He smiles. "I have a meeting in downtown Seattle in a couple of hours."

"Oh, is it fun downtown?"

"You've never been?"

"No." I shake my head and wish for another cup of coffee. "I've never been to the Pacific Northwest before."

"Wait." He holds up his hand, and a frown creases that handsome forehead. "You moved to a new city without ever having been here before? Why didn't you at least come out to see if you like it?"

"I couldn't afford to. I used all of my savings to rent this place. A trip here ahead of time wasn't possible. When Granddad died, I had to pay for his burial and stuff."

"He didn't have life insurance?" Zane asks.

"No. I found out scammers swindled him out of a lot of money. He was old and an easy mark. I feel guilty for that." I swallow hard at the memory of finding out that my grandfather had been taken advantage of. "He never told me. And I didn't live with him, so there was no way for me to know. Anyway, he was pretty much broke when he passed."

"I'm sorry, Aubrey."

I look over at him. He watches me with blue eyes full of...empathy?

"It could have been worse."

"Really? How so?"

"Are you kidding? He could have been in debt, too. Then I would have been responsible for everything. As it was, I just had to make sure he was taken care of, which was my job. He raised me."

"Where are your parents?" he asks.

"Dead." I shrug. "I don't remember them. Do you have your parents?"

"They're living, but I don't speak with them," he replies. "My best friend, Sabrina, is my family. She lives here in Seattle with her husband."

"Oh, nice. So, they're close by then. Are you filming a movie here?"

His lips twitch. "No."

I nod and look away, determined to mind my own damn business.

"I'm hiding," he says, surprising me.

"From what?"

Zane clears his throat and shifts in his chair. "Do you not keep up on pop culture?"

"Not really. I don't even have social media."

"Well, there was a scandal. There always is, really. But, this time, it was bad. My manager told me to get lost for a little while until it blows over."

"And your family is *here*." I nod. "That makes sense. But can I be honest?"

He sends me a wary look. "Sure."

"You're like...*Zane Cooper*. I picture you living in a big house with open spaces, a pool, and servants."

He smirks and then laughs. "I have that in LA. And I like it. There weren't any houses for lease in the area I want to be in. Rina and Ben live just down the way, so I can walk to their place. I like the area. And this condo is new, nicely furnished, and came with a surprise roommate."

I grimace. "I should have bowed out gracefully and found something else."

His eyes narrow. "Why?"

"Because you paid in advance for the whole time. And you got here first."

"So, finder's keepers?" He cocks a brow. "I don't think that works on homes, Aubrey."

I laugh. "Probably not. I'm grateful that you let me stay. At least, until the landlord refunds me the money I paid him. I told him that I knew he'd been double paid. He wasn't thrilled that I figured that out."

"But he *is* sending you a check, right?"

"That's what he said. And don't worry, I'll pay you for half of the rent."

He waves me off. "You don't have to worry about that."

"Uh, yeah. I do. And if you want me to, I'll look for something else."

He shakes his head slowly. "I don't mind if you stay. As long as you share your food."

"I thought you said you have a personal chef."

"Yeah, she's starting next week. She was on vacation this week. But you buy the good snacks. I'll have to spend more time at the gym, but that's okay. I have time."

"So, you're fine with me living here as long as I buy snacks?"

He shrugs. "Sure."

"Okay. Deal." I offer my hand to shake. He eyes it for a second and then folds his warm hand over mine. I feel a jolt.

Like, a physical shot of electricity the way it's described in romance novels.

His blue eyes narrow.

I feel mine widen.

"Okay, then." I pull my hand away and feel the loss. "I'd better get ready and get to the school—meet my boss, see my classroom. I hope you have a good day."

I pick up my leftover burrito and hurry inside. I fling the blanket on the bed, then quickly stow away my breakfast in the kitchen.

I hear Zane closing himself in his bedroom and rush back into mine, shutting the door.

Then I let out a long sigh.

All of the hype about how sexy Zane Cooper is isn't overblown. I can attest to that.

But he's my *roommate.* Maybe, eventually, he'll be my friend.

And the sooner I realize that that's it, the better. Because men like Zane Cooper don't have feelings for girls like me. It's just humiliation waiting to happen. He's being nice. He might like me, but that's all it will ever be.

* * * *

"This is your classroom." Winnie Winstead, the principal, flips on the lights and steps back so I can walk inside.

I immediately feel my heart sink.

It's an old building. The industrial carpet is worn. The small desks have all seen better days.

Not to mention, it's small and bare-bones.

"No books, no supplies?" I ask her. "Crayons and such?"

"It's just not in our budget," she says with an apologetic shrug. "We ask each student to bring a list of things. Most of them do."

But some don't. Because they can't afford to.

"Could you please send me the list that goes out to the parents?" I ask her.

"Of course. I'll do that as soon as I'm back at my desk. Feel free to do pretty much whatever you like in here. Anything will be an improvement. Welcome, Miss Stansfield. We're lucky to have you."

She smiles, and then I hear the click of her heels as she walks down the empty hallway back to her office.

I had hoped my room would be nicer. When I did some research on the elementary school, I discovered that part of it had been updated just two years ago.

Obviously, *my* room wasn't part of that remodel.

I sigh and turn a slow circle, taking it all in.

The windows are clean and give me a nice view of the courtyard at the center of the school. The big whiteboards look new, which is nice.

I take my bag over to my new desk, sit in the chair, and almost sink to the floor.

Looks like my desk chair is broken.

"I guess I know where the rest of my savings is going," I mumble to myself. I need more supplies than I realized. And a new chair.

I can request one, but that could take weeks. Maybe months.

If I absolutely have to, I can bust out my credit card, but I worked really hard to keep that baby at a zero balance.

I blow out a breath and then get to work.

An hour later, I have lists of what I need to buy, and the desks and chairs organized the way I like them.

Tomorrow, students and their parents can come by to meet me and to see their desks. And then the following day is the first day of school.

I'm not nervous. I thought I would be, but I'm not. I'm excited. I'm looking forward to getting the year underway. Meeting my kids and finally settling into a routine.

But first, I have a lot to do by tomorrow.

I want the room put together before the kids come in to meet me. So, I snatch up my purse and lists and go shopping.

* * * *

"I'm in and out," I say, out of breath as I hurry into the condo a few hours later. "I just have to grab some things, and then I'm headed to the school."

I run to my walk-in closet and grab the big tote bin I brought with me from Arizona. It has all of my favorite wall hangings for the classroom.

Then, I lug it back out of the apartment.

"I've got this," Zane says and relieves me of the tote, following me down to my car. "You're flushed. Are you okay?"

"I'm busy," I reply and push a lock of hair out of my eyes. "I have to set up my classroom tonight because the students are coming to meet me tomorrow. It's going to take a while, so I have to run. Thanks for your help."

I smile at him and drop back into my car. I shift into reverse, but

Zane knocks on my window.

"Yeah?" I ask after rolling it down.

"I can come help."

I scowl. "You don't need to do that. I've got it. Just don't wait up."

"That's it. Do *not* move this car."

He jogs back up the steps to the apartment, and I check the time. It's already mid-afternoon. Time is slipping by.

But he quickly returns, jogs to my passenger door, and climbs into the vehicle.

"I had to grab my wallet," he informs me.

"Zane, this is silly. You don't have to do this."

"Do you think that I *can't* help?"

"Of course, not."

"Then off we go." He taps his fingers on his knees and raises a brow when I don't move. "Are we going or what?"

"If you get bored, I can bring you home."

"Aubrey?"

"Yeah?"

"*Now* you're annoying me."

I laugh and pull out of the parking space, heading for the school. We make our way through empty hallways to my classroom, and I usher him inside.

"This is it."

Zane sets the tote down, and I pile my bags next to it.

"It's pretty...institutional," he decides.

"I'm going to make it look so cute, the kids won't even notice that it's old and dingy. I bought all kinds of things, along with extra supplies to keep stored for when someone runs short. Some kids just can't bring everything on the supply list."

Zane frowns down at me. "So, you buy it all? Like, out of your own pocket?"

"Yeah." I prop my hands on my hips and consider the wall space above the dry-erase board. "I think I'll put my alphabet up there."

"You have socks in this bag," Zane says with a confused frown.

"Yeah, I keep extra things like that, too. Socks and underwear. You never know when there will be an accident. They're only six, Zane."

"Okay. What do you want me to do?"

"I'm going to use you for your height. I need some things hung."

"I'm at your service."

Chapter Four

~Zane~

"Oh my God."

She's trying to make her voice stern, but I can hear the giggle fighting its way out of her.

Making Aubrey laugh is quickly becoming my new hobby.

I stand back from the wall, hands on my hips, and survey my handiwork.

Aubrey tasked me with hanging the alphabet on the wall above the whiteboard. She didn't say what *order* to hang it in.

So, I might have arranged the letters into swear words. Just to startle her.

"They have to learn sooner or later."

She covers her mouth with her hand, but she can't hide the laughter.

We've been at this for several hours. Hanging colorful animals and other things all over the walls. Organizing furniture and everything else she brought in with her earlier.

But even I can see that it's still pretty bare in here.

"I'll buy more here and there," she says as if she can read my mind. "I want to get some plastic bins to set over there for books and educational toys. In a perfect world, I'd buy a small fridge to keep snacks. I'm not a daycare, but kids learn better if they're not hungry. And too many kids go hungry."

I have the undeniable urge to reach out and touch her. Aubrey has a soft heart, especially for kids. Hell, she'd spend every penny she earns on the children if she could.

"You remind me of Sabrina," I say and wrap my arm around her shoulders. I feel her stiffen and then relax next to me. "She runs a pantry in central Oregon, and a new one here in the Seattle area for kids. She provides snacks and meals and even feminine hygiene stuff for the girls."

"That's *amazing*," Aubrey says with excitement. "I wonder if she needs more volunteers. I'd be happy to help with that."

"I'm sure she could use the help." I frown as she pulls away to tug the cap off a black marker and write her name, *MISS STANSFIELD*, in all caps on the board. "Will they be able to read that?"

"No, but I'll teach them." She sighs and pushes her hand through her hair. It's amazing how it changes color in different light. This morning, on the balcony, it was sable brown. And this evening, under the fluorescent lights, I can see lighter highlights running through it.

"I like your hair."

She stops moving and stares at me with wide eyes. "My hair?"

I nod slowly.

"It's just mousy brown. I really should find a place to get it worked on, but I haven't had time."

"I like it," I repeat and close the few steps between us so I can hook a soft strand behind her ear.

She shivers.

I grin down at her.

"I guess we can't forget to rearrange those letters," she says and licks her lips.

"Do I make you nervous?"

"Don't you make *everyone* nervous?"

I smile softly. "No."

The women I've known lately are too confident, in an egocentric, arrogant way that isn't flattering to them. They just don't hold my interest.

Aubrey, though, is sweet and...*normal*. She's an attractive woman who makes me feel good when I'm with her.

"When you're not arranging my letters into crude, inappropriate words—which I admit is funny—you're a little intimidating."

"Because of my celebrity status?"

Her mouth opens and then closes again. "Well, of course. Yes. But also because you're—" She gestures vaguely to me. "You're *that*."

"I'm what?"

"You know what."

God, she makes me laugh. "I don't. Use your words, Aubrey."

A startled giggle escapes her, and she shakes her head. "You're hot, Zane."

I gasp and clutch at my non-existent pearls. "Me? Hot?"

She rolls her eyes and drags the stepladder over to start rearranging my letters. When she's three steps up, I'm at eye-level with her breasts.

Not a bad place to be if I'm honest.

"Hold these." She takes letters down and passes them to me. She's up and down on the stool as she has to move it side to side to put the letters on the wall. I should take over for her, but damn it, I like seeing her move on and off the ladder.

Fifteen minutes later, the letters are arranged in the correct order, and when Aubrey turns to get down, she stumbles, falling forward. I wrap my arms around her middle to catch her.

My face plants right in her cleavage, and her arms wrap around my neck.

We don't move for a good five seconds.

"I'm so sorry," she says and pushes her hands against my shoulders. I let her slide slowly to the floor, but I don't loosen my grasp on her.

"Easy there." I watch her mouth as she licks those lips once more. I want to taste them. I want to feel her move and moan under me, more than I've ever wanted anything else. "Aubrey, I'd like to kiss you."

"Oh." Her brown eyes widen, and her breath quickens.

Jesus, I can't resist her.

"If you'd rather I didn't, I need you to say so, honey."

"It's okay. If you want to."

Being given the green light has never sounded so damn good. I slowly lower my head and brush my lips against hers gently. Once, twice. And then I *kiss* her. Not too deep or too intensely, but enough to make it clear that I enjoy it very much—so much that I'd love to boost her up against the wall and sink inside of her. Make her squirm in delight.

When I pull away, I rest my forehead on hers, and we both take a deep breath.

"So, let me get this straight," she says and looks me in the eyes. "You're hot, *and* you're a grade-A kisser? I don't think that's fair. There should be a rule against that somewhere."

I grin and kiss her forehead. "It takes two to make a good kiss."

"Yeah, well." She doesn't say anything else as she pulls back and presses her fingers to her lips. "I think I'm done for tonight. It's getting late, and I have to be back here by eight tomorrow morning."

"Let's go, then," I say and help her get the room locked up. "Are you hungry?"

"So hungry," she confirms. "Let's order pizza or something. I don't want to go sit in a restaurant. I'm probably stinky after all of that work."

She turns a horrified look my way after starting the car.

"Oh, God. Do I stink?"

She smells her armpits and makes me laugh.

"No. You don't stink. You're funny, you know that?"

"Funny-looking," she says as if it's an automatic response that she's used for years.

I don't like it. Not one bit.

"What do you like on your pizza?" She flips on her turn signal and looks at me expectantly. "I usually go for plain ol' pepperoni, but I'm flexible. Except when it comes to mushrooms. I don't eat fungus."

"I like *only* mushrooms on my pizza."

She rolls her eyes and lets out a gusty sigh. "Liar."

I grin. I love it that she calls me out on my shit. That she treats me like a normal person.

"Pepperoni works for me. Should we pretend we're adults and also get a salad? Eat a vegetable?"

"If you insist." She parks her car in her spot, and we get out, making our way up to our condo.

"Why don't you go get comfortable, and I'll order the pizza?" I suggest. She yawns, lifts her arms over her head, and sniffs an armpit again.

"Good idea. I *am* a little ripe. I'll just take a shower."

"Do you prefer regular or thin crust?" I call after her as she walks down the hallway.

"Surprise me," she answers.

Oh, I could surprise her with all sorts of things. In fact, if surprises are her thing, I can have fun with that.

But for tonight, I'll start with the pizza.

I text Rina to ask what the best pizza is around here, then place an order. Surprisingly, they tell me that it should arrive in thirty minutes, so I change my clothes and get comfortable myself, pouring a glass of wine, and flipping on the gas fireplace in the living room. I just sat down to get comfortable when Aubrey comes walking into the room, her hair wet and in a pile on her head. She's wearing an oversize, black T-shirt over black leggings, and her feet are bare.

"There's an open bottle of wine on the counter," I offer.

"Perfect."

She pours herself a glass and sits on the couch across from me, her feet pulled up under her, and sighs in happiness.

"Much better," she says and sips her wine. "Being a teacher is a lot of physical work. You wouldn't think so, but it is."

"Oh, I think it's probably one of the hardest jobs there is," I reply and rub my hand over my chin. "How many kids will you have in your class?"

"Twenty-eight." She winces and then shrugs one shoulder. "It's a lot in one classroom. I prefer twenty or less so I can give each child more of my attention."

"Will you have an aid or a helper of some kind?"

"Not that I've been told." She sighs. "Sometimes, we get student teachers from the colleges, who need to put in classroom hours. That can be a big help. Other times, I get parents who want to come in and help. They'll read or just work one-on-one with kids who need a little extra attention. It'll work out. This is a good school system. I know my classroom looks old, but they're slowly remodeling the whole building. I'm looking forward to meeting my kiddos tomorrow and getting the year started."

"When did you decide to be a teacher?" I ask her, just as the doorbell rings. "Hold that thought."

I set down my wine and hurry to the door. I take the boxes handed to me, sign a slip, and then shut the door, carrying the food to the kitchen.

"I'll come help."

"You sit." I point to her and then load up two plates with pizza, breadsticks, and salad, carrying them into the living room with napkins before settling across from her once more. "Okay. When did you decide to be a teacher?"

She takes a bite of salad and chews, thinking it over. "I was in high school. In the summer, I got a job at a daycare. I really loved working with the older kids. Babies are fine, but it was the older ones that I took an interest in. And then I just knew. It was pretty organic, I guess you could say. When did you know you wanted to be an actor?"

I frown down at my plate. "I don't remember a time when I *wasn't* an actor. My parents got me into the business before I could walk. So not being an actor wasn't an option."

She frowns. "What if you hated it?"

"I did, for a while. Especially when I was younger, and the paparazzi wouldn't leave me alone. I couldn't do *anything* without having a camera in my face."

"You couldn't be a kid," she says softly. "Just a regular person."

"No. But don't feel sorry for me. I have a pretty great life."

She smiles and bites into her pizza, then groans in happiness.

Fucking hell, I want to hear her groan like that when I'm inside of her.

"If I'd known this pizza was here," she says, swallows, and takes another bite, "I would have moved here a long time ago."

"Wow, pizza is what does it, huh?"

"This is excellent pizza. Anyway, I don't feel sorry for you. I do feel bad that you didn't have more of a normal upbringing. But everyone's life experience is different, right? Mine was very...ordinary. Parents died in an accident when I was a baby. Grandpa raised me. Grew up in a small town in Arizona. There's really nothing extraordinary about me. Just a different life experience."

"There are plenty of things about you that make you special, Aubrey."

Her cheeks redden, and she frowns. "Anyway, what's your favorite movie? Not one you were in, but one you like to watch the best."

"You don't like hearing that you're special."

"I'm not fishing for compliments, Zane. Look, I know who I am, okay? I'm the homely girl that people look at sideways, don't really care to get to know, and pretty much ignore. I'm just...*plain*. And that's okay. Don't *you* feel sorry for *me*."

I want to punch anyone who's ever told her that she's not special.

I want to tell her all the ways I think she's amazing.

But it'll only make her uncomfortable. I don't want to do that. We've had a good day, and I'm enjoying her.

I want to kiss her again.

"*To Kill a Mockingbird*."

"Huh?"

"My favorite movie is *To Kill a Mockingbird*. The book is fabulous, too, but man, Gregory Peck could *act*. I love everything about that film."

"I've never seen it."

I lower my pizza to my plate and stare at her as if she just said that she's been possessed by a ghost and wants me to do the cha-cha.

"Never?"

"Nope." She nibbles on a piece of garlic bread. "But now I want to."

"Oh, it's going to happen. You have to see it. Did you read the book?"

"Yes, in high school. But I was sick the day they watched the movie in class. So, I missed it."

I already have an idea forming in my head on how to remedy this. I'll make some calls in the morning.

"Oh, how did your meeting go today?" she asks. "I'm sorry, I should have asked you earlier."

"It was great, actually. Do you know who Luke Williams is?"

She frowns. "Wasn't he in those vampire movies?"

"Yes, forever ago. He's a producer now. Owns a studio. It's based here in Seattle because he lives here with his family. Anyway, I'm going to be in Washington for about six months, and I can't sit idle. I'd go crazy. I need to work or *something*."

"I get that. I love having the summer off, but I'm always ready to go back to work."

"Exactly. I think I might take on a directing role in a TV show his company produces."

"Wow, that's awesome! Congratulations."

"Thanks." Somehow, Aubrey's pride and enthusiasm in my work is more satisfying than winning a damn Oscar. "It's a new challenge, but I'm up for it. I've considered directing for years, but I've always been busy with acting. This is the first break I've had in a long, long time."

"I do notice that you are in a lot of movies," she says with a nod. "But that's good. It means you have work. You won't go hungry."

I laugh and then nod. "You're right. I won't. Okay, your turn. What's your favorite movie?"

"*Captain America.*"

I blink at her. "I was in that one."

"You were?" Her eyes widen as if she's shocked. "I had no idea."

"Sarcasm. You're being sarcastic, aren't you?"

She giggles and sets her empty plate aside. "I love superhero movies. The action, the lessons, the right conquering wrong. I just like it."

And I like her.

A lot.

Maybe too much. Because she's rooted here in Seattle now, and in six months, I'm leaving. She's not the kind of girl you sleep with for the short term and then bail—no harm, no foul.

And I can't give her the kind of relationship that sticks.

But damn if I'm not completely taken with her.

"You have a funny look on your face. Does it make it awkward that one of *your* movies is my favorite?"

"I think it would make it awkward if one of my movies *wasn't* your favorite."

I give her an arrogant smile.

She rolls her eyes. "Yeah, okay. You're just a little full of yourself, Zane."

I laugh and cross my arms over my chest, enjoying her. "But you like me."

"Eh. You're okay."

Chapter Five

~Aubrey~

It's been the longest week of my life.

I'm almost finished with the first week of school, and I'm exhausted. The kids are tough. Some of the parents have been a downright nightmare.

I want a drink and my bed for forty-eight hours straight.

"I don't want to tie my own shoes," Timmy says with a scowl. "You do it."

"We all have to tie our own shoes," I reply and shake my head. "You know how. I saw you do it earlier today."

"*You're* the teacher," Timmy says, holding his ground. "It's your job. My dad pays taxes, so you get paid, and you're supposed to do it."

I raise a brow. Obviously, Timmy hears all kinds of colorful things at home.

If I give into him during the first week, he will make my life hell all year.

I squat next to him. "Do you like Captain America?" I ask and point to his T-shirt that sports the superhero's shield.

"Sure."

"I do, too. He's a nice guy, right? He's respectful. And I'm pretty sure he ties his own shoes."

Timmy frowns and then sighs as if it's the biggest chore in the world. Still, he gets to work tying his laces.

"Are you always going to be mean?" a little girl named Bella asks.

"I'm not mean at all."

"We didn't have to tie our own shoes in kindergarten," someone else informs me. "You're just mean. And you didn't let us have a snack."

"We did have snacks." I sigh and rub my hand over my face.

Stay calm. It's the end of the day. You get to go home now.

"Hello, darling."

"Mom!" Timmy jumps up and runs into his mother's arms. I inwardly cringe.

Martha has been in my classroom every blessed day this week, and it's mostly been to complain.

"Mom, Miss Stansfield is mean."

Martha's gaze flies to my face, and her eyes narrow.

Here we go.

"Why is that?" Martha asks her son.

"She wouldn't tie my shoes."

I smile in that patient way I learned to do when I started this career. "Timmy, we all tie our own shoes. You know that."

"I don't see why you couldn't just help him," Martha says, completely eradicating everything I managed to do over the past fifteen minutes. "It only takes a second."

"Bye, Miss S!"

Several kids wave as they leave the room, excited to meet their bus or find their parents, picking them up.

A few lag behind, putting on shoes and jackets.

Martha is still glaring at me.

"We have a rule," I say calmly. "All of us ties our own shoes."

"You're not nice like Captain America," Timmy spits out. "I bet no one likes you. I bet you don't have any friends."

"Actually," I say before I can stop myself, "I *live* with Captain America."

If I could pull the words back, I would. But they're out now, and there's nothing I can do about it.

"Really?" a little boy named Robert says in excitement.

"I want to meet him," Ashley says.

"Now you're lying to the children?" Martha says with disgust. "I'm calling the principal. I don't want my child in a liar's classroom."

She grabs Timmy's hand and storms away. I usher the last of the kids out, close my classroom door, and sigh.

"Go home," I tell myself. "Just forget about everything until

Monday. There's no need to get all riled up."

I close up my room for the weekend and set off on foot toward my condo. It's not far, and I've enjoyed the walks each day.

But the more I walk, the more worked up I get. I hope she *does* take Timmy out of my class. He's a little jerk. He disrupts my lessons, he's needy, and he's spoiled. Having him moved wouldn't hurt my feelings in the least.

But I'm not a liar. That comment pissed me off.

Not that I can prove it.

Oh, God, what did I do? I might have just thrown my roommate under the bus. He's going to kill me.

My heart is hammering as I push into the condo and make a beeline for the kitchen. I drop my bag on the floor, shimmy out of my coat, and toss it on a chair, then open the fridge for the other half-bottle of wine from the other night.

I pull off the stopper and drink directly from the bottle.

"Uh, hi."

I freeze and turn to find Zane watching me curiously from the living room.

"Hi," I say after I finish the bottle. I toss it into the recycling bin and pull another out of the fridge, reaching for the corkscrew.

"Bad day?"

"Bad week." I'm trying to twist the sucker into the cork, but my hands are too shaky, and I can't get it right. "Damn it, why is the universe against me?"

"I got it," he says smoothly, taking the bottle from me and then opening it. "But before you get hammered on wine, do you want to talk about it?"

"No." I snatch the bottle and take a sip, making him wince. I start to pace around the kitchen, back and forth. "Okay, yeah. I do. These kids are feral. They're *mean*. And their language is appalling. Little bullies."

I drink more wine and keep pacing.

"And don't even get me started on their parents. A few have been nice, but for the most part, they're just rude. You're not going to like this part. You might kick me out. You might hate me."

His eyebrow flings up. "Did you call the paparazzi?"

That stops me in my tracks, and I frown. "No. Of course, not. I'm an idiot, not an asshole."

"Okay, what happened?"

"This kid, Timmy, is such a little jerk. He was goading me, and his mom was there, and the next thing I knew, I was telling him that I live with Captain America."

I drink again, unable to look Zane in the eyes.

"But don't worry. His mother called me a liar and told me she's taking her kid out of my class because she doesn't want him learning from a liar. So, they probably don't believe me."

"You're not a liar," he says with a scowl. "And I'm pissed that she called you one."

"Yeah, well, you should be pissed that I told someone you live here. Because that's not cool. I know you're lying low. It just *happened*. Because he was wearing a Captain America shirt, and...oh, hell. I don't know."

I finally sit on a stool in defeat.

"I'm going to have to quit my job. I would go throw myself off a bridge, but I have too much left to live for. I've never even had *sex* for fuck's sake. I want to know what that's like. So, instead, I'll just quit my job and go sell handmade necklaces on the beach in Mexico."

"Wait." Zane holds up a hand and then pulls that same palm down his face. "There is so much to unpack there. I don't even know where to start."

"I'm just babbling." I shrug and take another sip. I'm starting to feel the buzz, and it's welcome.

"Back up to the sex part. You've never had it?"

"Shit, did I say that out loud?"

"Yes. You did."

I blow out a breath through my lips, making a raspberry sound. "If you *must* know, no. I've never done it. But I will. Someday, when I'm not dealing with six-year-old bullies."

There's a knock on our door.

"Shit, is that Timmy's dad, here to bust my ass for saying that I live with you?"

"No, drama queen, that's the chef here to drop off dinner."

Zane laughs as he opens the door. In walks a *gorgeous* woman, carrying a big, insulated bag, which Zane takes from her.

"Hey there, handsome," she says with a wink. Her smile dims when she sees me. "Oh, hello."

"Hey." I nod at her and take another swig from the bottle. Her eyes widen. "It's been a hell of a week."

"I guess so. I'm Amy. I'll be bringing in meals for you two. Tonight, we're starting with…"

She starts to ramble about whatever she cooked and gives Zane instructions to just pop it in the oven if we're not ready for it now.

"It'll actually pair really well with that wine you're drinking."

"Awesome."

Zane walks Amy to the door, where she assures him that she's only a phone call away if he needs anything at all.

I smirk.

"What?" he says after he shuts the door.

"She's hoping you need *her*. She practically threw herself at you."

"No, I've seen throwing plenty of times, and that wasn't it. She was just hinting."

"She nearly pushed her boobs against your chest." I sniff the air and have to admit, it smells good. "If you go for the fake triple-D types."

"Are you jealous?"

"No, I'm irritated. And not even with Amy. I'm just tired, and I'm failing at my job. And maybe I shouldn't have had so much wine."

"Okay, okay." Zane slides dinner into the oven, then comes around the island to wrap his arms around me. "It's hard to start a new job. And kids are difficult. Take a deep breath. Why don't you go take a shower and get comfy? Then we'll eat our weight in pasta."

"There's pasta?" I sniffle.

"Didn't you hear her?"

"No, I didn't pay attention. Actually, we should do that in the other order. Eat, then shower. Because I think I need that pasta to soak up some of this wine."

"Good idea."

* * * *

An hour later, my belly is full, I'm fresh from the shower, and I feel a lot better. Zane made me laugh during dinner and then told me to go shower while he cleaned up.

He's handy to have around.

Honestly, he's nice. So much nicer than I expected.

And he's hotter than hell.

I still can't believe I told him that I'm a virgin.

I walk out of my bedroom to get something to drink from the kitchen. When I'm on my way back to my room, I see that his bedroom door is open, and he's sitting on his bed, watching TV.

I wander over to his door and lean on the doorjamb. He smiles when he looks my way. His eyes roam over my simple white tank and red boxer shorts and seem to gleam when he looks back up at my eyes.

"Do you feel better?"

"Yeah. I do, thanks. What are you watching?"

"Early episodes of the show I'm going to direct."

I nod and glance at the TV. I've never seen this one. It's a medical drama.

"Do you mind if I join you?"

"Not at all." He scoots a little to the side, and I climb up onto the bed with him, set my drink aside, and we watch the show for a few silent minutes.

"Here, give me your foot," he says, holding out his hand.

"For what?"

"I'm going to rub it, Aubrey."

"Oh. Well, then." I shift so I can put my feet in his lap. When he pushes his thumb into the arch, I have to bite my lip so I don't groan out loud.

Good God, this man is good with his hands.

"You're on your feet a lot," he says quietly.

"Part of the job." I sigh. I can't help it. My eyes feel a little heavy, and my stomach tightens when his hands travel up my calf to massage the muscles there.

My body always comes to life when he's around. When he kissed me in my classroom, I almost died from the pleasure of it.

I didn't want him to stop.

I may be inexperienced, but I know what feels good when it's happening, and Zane makes me feel *good*.

"Oh, I forgot to ask you," he says as he pulls his fingers firmly down my shin. "Luke asked me to join him and his wife for dinner tomorrow night. I'd like for you to come with me."

"Like, as your date?"

His grin is quick. "Yeah. As my date."

That gives me butterflies on top of the butterflies I already had. "But I don't really have anything to wear, Zane. I'm not an eat-out-with-rich-people kind of girl."

"Just people," he says with a shrug. "And it's not fancy. I'll be wearing jeans. You'll look great in anything."

I want to smirk, but the magical things he's doing with his hands makes it impossible.

"It's just dinner out. You'll like them. Luke and Natalie are great."

"Okay. Just don't ever stop doing that."

"Did you wear this outfit to purposefully seduce me?" he asks, and my eyes snap open in surprise.

"What? No. This is a ratty old tank and boxers. It's not exactly seduction material."

"Sexiest thing I've ever seen," he mutters, and his hands start to roam farther up my leg. "I don't want to come off as a creep here. And I want to take things easy. Slow."

"Hold up." I cover his hand with mine. When he holds my gaze, I say, "Are you doing this because I said I'm a virgin, and now you think I'm some sort of weird conquest?"

He barks out a laugh and shakes his head. "God, I love how honest you are. No. Not at all. I've been attracted to you since you challenged me to rock, paper, scissors. And when we were in your classroom last week, I wanted to do way more than just kiss you."

"Me, too," I whisper and watch as his blue eyes darken.

"You can say no," he says softly.

"Who would say no to Captain America?"

His eyes narrow. "That's not who I am, Aubrey. I'm *Zane*. Just Zane. With you."

I feel stupid for saying that. Of course, it was a ridiculous thing to say, but before I can apologize, he leans in and brushes his lips over mine.

"Say it," he says as he skims his nose across my cheek. "Say my name."

"Zane." I swallow hard when he smiles against my ear.

"I like the way you say my name." Those magical hands of his roam over my arms, and one hand cups my breast. "If you are *ever* uncomfortable, you just say so, Aubrey."

I sigh.

"Did you hear me?"

I nod.

"I need to hear the words, baby."

"I'll say something." My voice is rough, so different than I've ever heard it before. And my God, I want him. I want all of him.

His fingers are just *everywhere*. Suddenly, they're inside my boxer shorts.

"You're not wearing panties under there," he says in surprise.

"No." I push my fingers through his soft hair. "I'm not."

He moans, but he doesn't touch me *there*. Not yet. He's too busy touching me everywhere else. When he pulls the tank over my head and lays me flat on my back, I don't even have time to be self-conscious before he grins and leans in to kiss my breast.

Whose life is this? Am I dreaming?

Surely, I'm dreaming.

I'm not about to have sex with Zane Cooper.

Except, I think I am.

And it's not because he's a megastar actor. It's because he's funny, nice to me, and just a good human.

I *like* him for who he is.

And I know without a doubt that he likes me, too.

"You have the softest skin," he murmurs as he trails a line of kisses down my belly. I want to cover my pouch there, but he just kisses it and keeps going happily along as if he doesn't mind my curves at all.

His mouth journeys back up to my neck, and then my lips as his hands slide my shorts down my legs. With his eyes on mine, his fingers get to work in that most sensitive area.

"Oh, Zane."

"That's right." He smiles softly. "God, I fucking love my name on your tongue. Say it again."

His fingers move in and then out and over, making me so damn wet. I bite my lip and close my eyes, but he tugs my lip out of my teeth with his free hand.

"Say it," he instructs me again.

"Zane." It's a gasp now. I can't stop moving my legs. My hips. "Zane, I need—"

"What?" He kisses my cheek. The corner of my lips. "What do you need? Tell me."

"You. Inside of me. God, Zane, I need you inside of me."

"I have to grab—" He leans over, and I hear the drawer open. When I look, he has a foil packet in his hand. He opens it with his teeth, shifts around, and then nudges my legs apart with his hips.

"I didn't even get to play with it," I pout, but he laughs and kisses me long and slow.

"I'd make a fool of myself if you did that right now," he says. "But there will be plenty of opportunities. Now, this might be a little uncomfortable, but I promise you, I'm going to be gentle and slow. There's no hurry. Just tell me if you want me to stop."

I cup his face in my hands and smile up at him. "I'm not scared, Zane."

His lips twitch. "Good. That's one of us."

I blink. My jaw drops. I can't believe how full he makes me feel, how *alive*. When he's seated fully, he brushes my hair off my cheek and kisses me sweetly.

"How you doing?"

"Holy shit."

He grins. "Yeah?"

"Oh, yeah. Are you going to move now?"

"Impatient." He links my hand with his, kisses my fingers, and then clutches our hands between us against his chest as he starts to move. It's slow at first, but then he sets a rhythm that makes my heart pound and sets my nerves on fire.

It doesn't hurt at all, and I feel a pressure building inside of me. It's a fire. An *inferno*. And when he pushes deep and rubs himself against that most sensitive spot, I come apart beneath him, calling his name in either desperation or as a prayer, I don't know which.

He groans into my ear, tenses, and shivers.

And I know, in this moment, that no matter what happens later between the two of us, I'll never be the same.

Chapter Six

~Zane~

She's nervous, and I don't blame her. But I don't want her to be uncomfortable all night. I want Aubrey to have a good time with Luke and Nat. They're some of the best people I know.

"You're gorgeous," I say as I wrap my arms around her waist from behind and smile at her in the master bathroom mirror. She's teased her hair into some curls, and her outfit hugs her body perfectly. "I'm telling you, it's not a fancy dinner. You don't have to get all gussied up."

"This isn't gussied up," she insists and brushes on some mascara. "This is just normal I'm-going-to-be-around-people stuff. It's good that I don't have to get fancy because I don't own fancy."

"You look great," I repeat.

"And you're very sweet."

I sigh and kiss her neck. I haven't been able to keep my hands off her since last night, and she doesn't seem to mind.

I hadn't planned to have sex with her. Especially after she said she was a virgin.

No way.

But there is just something about her that I can't resist. No, she's not movie-star gorgeous. But, frankly, I've *had* that kind of girl—more than once.

That's not for me.

Aubrey is fun and smart, and she can kiss like crazy. Her body is smooth and soft and responsive. Her laugh lights me up. Her smile can bring me to my knees.

And don't even get me started on the noises this girl makes when my hands are on her, and I'm making her go wild.

If I think about that too much, I'll just haul her back to bed and cancel on Luke.

"Why are you watching me?" she asks at last.

"I like watching you."

She snorts, shakes her head, and runs her fingers through her hair.

"Okay, well, I think this is as good as it's going to get tonight."

I move in to kiss her, but she pulls back.

"No way. No messing me up."

I narrow my eyes but then nod. "I look forward to messing you up later, then."

She laughs, grabs her bag, and we head out to my car. The trip into the city doesn't take long. Eventually, we end up at a restaurant on the waterfront.

She fidgets in the seat next to me, so I reach over and cover her hand with mine.

"You're going to like them. Really."

"Yeah." She blows out a nervous breath. "Okay."

* * * *

"I like her," Luke murmurs to me as Natalie and Aubrey chat and laugh across from us. They've had their heads together all through dinner as if they're old friends.

"Me, too." I sip my wine and watch the two women. "Natalie's good at making people feel at ease."

"She's had a lot of practice," Luke replies. "And it's part of her nature. What's happening there, between the two of you?"

I shrug a shoulder. "Honestly, I don't know for sure yet. I like her. She's fresh and fun. Sweet, you know?"

"Yeah. I know. She's not what you're used to."

"Not at all. And it's so refreshing."

"Oh my gosh, Aubrey, we're having a girls' night out next weekend at my house," Natalie says, catching my attention. "My cousin, Amelia, is about to launch a brand-new makeup line, and we get a sneak peek at it all. So, there will be makeovers and martinis and probably some cupcakes involved. I'd love it if you came."

Aubrey blinks in surprise. "Oh, well, thank you. That does sound like fun."

"It's probably too much fun," Natalie admits. "But don't worry, it's completely safe, and everyone is just great."

"Is this Amelia Montgomery we're talking about?" Aubrey asks.

"That's right."

"I'm wearing her mascara tonight," Aubrey says. "I love her stuff."

"Well, this is perfect, then." Natalie grins. "Have Zane drive you. The lemon drop martinis are strong."

Aubrey laughs and then looks over at me. "I might need a chauffeur next weekend."

"I'm happy to," I reply. "Sounds like fun—if you're a girl."

Luke laughs, and Natalie narrows her eyes.

"Good thing I'm a girl," Aubrey says and smiles at the waiter as he approaches.

"Can I interest you in dessert?" he asks.

"Yes." Aubrey nods. "Dessert is always a yes."

"Oh, I like you," Natalie says, also nodding at the waiter.

"I'll bring the tray so you can see tonight's selections," he says and walks away.

"You and I are going to be good friends," Natalie says to Aubrey, who just beams back at the other woman.

"What can I bring on Saturday?"

"Just yourself," Natalie replies. "We have everything else handled."

* * * *

"Okay, you were right," Aubrey says when we walk into the condo a couple of hours later. She slips out of her shoes and takes off her earrings. "They're really nice. And, somehow, I got invited to a girls'-night-out party. I'm not even sure what that entails, but I'm really looking forward to it."

"I don't have any idea what it involves, either." I pull her against me. "Men aren't allowed to know what happens at those things. I don't think I *want* to know."

She laughs and kisses my chin. "You were charming tonight."

"Really? How so?"

"You're just a good conversationalist. You're good with people. And you're not a jerk."

"I used to be," I admit. "There was a time that I had an ego the size of Beverly Hills and could be a punk. Mostly, I learned that I was angry. And I had no right to be, really. So, I got some therapy, and I'm not such a jerk anymore."

"I'm glad I didn't know you during your jerk phase," she says. "Because then I wouldn't be interested in living with you. Or kissing you."

I quirk a brow. "Oh? Are you interested in kissing me?"

She smiles but then shrugs as if it doesn't matter. "Maybe."

"Is it just kissing you're interested in?"

"You have so many questions," she replies. "Maybe you should just kiss me, and we'll see where it goes from there."

"You're a smart woman." I lean in and kiss her. Just a peck. "How was that?"

"How about this?"

She boosts herself up and plants one on me. She's not at all as shy as she was, and her confidence is its own aphrodisiac.

My body tightens. My dick hardens.

And when she pulls back and raises her eyebrows in question, I simply pick her up and march to her bedroom.

"I guess that was better," she says and laughs when I toss her onto the bed.

* * * *

"It's not a good idea," Hugh says into my ear. When I made the calls for my idea today, word traveled back to my manager, and he's been trying to talk me out of it ever since.

"It's already been set into motion," I inform him and check the rearview mirror to make sure the truck behind me is still there.

It is.

"But you're supposed to be lying *low*," he reminds me. "This isn't lying low, Zane."

"It's one classroom. We didn't alert the media. I want to do this for her, Hugh. I'm not giving out my address. I'm not doing anything shady. Stop worrying so much. If anything, if this gets out, it will *help* my reputation because I'm doing something nice."

I hear him blow out a breath in resignation.

"I'll be in touch."

He clicks off, and I pull into a parking space in the lot by Aubrey's school. I already cleared this with the principal, but I asked for confidentiality. Which, she assured me, she'd respect.

We'll see if she's a liar or if she holds true to her word.

"Thanks, guys. You can follow with the boxes. Just wait outside the classroom door until I give you the signal."

"Can do. Man, I wish I'd been in this classroom as a kid."

I grin at the delivery driver named Mack and lead them into the school and down the hall to Aubrey's room.

So far, it's quiet. Everyone's in class. It looks like the principal was good to her word and kept my plan to herself.

I open Aubrey's door and poke my head in.

"Miss Stansfield?"

She turns in surprise and then frowns, glancing at her students and then back to me. "What are you doing here?"

"Well, I heard there was a debate going about whether or not you know me."

I step inside, and the kids start to murmur, point, and someone even says, "That's Captain America!"

I grin at them, wink, and then turn back to Aubrey. "And I brought you these."

I pass a bouquet of pink roses to her and smile when she narrows her eyes at me, then buries her nose in a bloom.

"Holy crap," a little boy says in awe.

"Is that him?" I whisper to Aubrey.

"Yep."

I turn and squat next to Timmy. "Hey there."

"Uh, hi." His cheeks get red. "Sir."

"I've heard some things about you."

He looks down as if he's ashamed of himself. "Yeah."

"Miss Stansfield tells me that you're smart and clever and fun to be around."

His head whips back up, and he stares at me with wide eyes. Then he looks over at Aubrey. "She said that?"

"Sure. She also said that sometimes you get mad."

"I guess I do." He shrugs a little shoulder. "Sometimes."

"It's okay to get mad." I pat that shoulder. "But it's not okay to be mean. Nobody likes a mean guy, right?"

"Yeah, I suppose."

"I know you'll do better. You're a good kid, Timmy." I stand and smile at everyone. "Now, I didn't want to just bring Miss Stansfield a gift and leave the rest of you out, so I have some things to share."

I turn and signal for Mack to come in with the boxes.

For the next hour, I sit with each child, offer them all kinds of merchandise, pose for photos that Aubrey takes and promises to send to their parents.

"I love you," a little girl named Chloe says with the most sincere face I've ever seen. She wraps her small arms around my neck and gives me a squeeze.

"Aww, I love you, too, Chloe."

"You'd better go before school is out," Aubrey whispers to me. I nod, understanding that the school is about to be full of parents and other students, and I'd rather not be the center of attention for that.

I'm just thrilled that we were able to pull *this* off.

I look over the room of grinning faces. Some pulled shirts or sweatshirts over their clothes. Others hold dolls and backpacks. All of the merch was a big hit.

"I have to go, guys. You be good, okay?"

"Okay!"

"We will!"

"Thank you!"

They all yell in excitement and wave as I leave the room, hurrying out to my car. I slip away without seeing even *one* parent or member of the media.

I pulled it off.

Chapter Seven

~Aubrey~

He surprised my kids.

He came to my classroom with *gifts* and spent a good chunk of his afternoon with them. He was patient and sweet. He made each of them feel respected and important. And watching their eyes light up, well…it was the best day of my teaching career.

Maybe the best day of my life.

The kids were so excited when their parents came to collect them after school, though if it weren't for the official merchandise and the photos I sent to each of them, I'm pretty sure they wouldn't have believed it.

Of course, there's always that one person who tries to ruin everything, which just so happened to be Timmy's mom in this case. She scowled and asked me why I didn't get permission from the parents for a stranger to come see their kids, and I just smiled at her and said, "Bless your heart."

And I'm not even Southern.

I was not willing to let her ruin the wonderful thing that Zane did for those kids.

I climb the steps to our condo. When I open the door, I find Zane in the kitchen.

I don't even bother saying anything. I just rush over to him and launch myself into his arms.

"Does this mean that it was okay that I just showed up at your job today?"

I laugh and kiss his cheek, his neck, and then his lips. I lock my legs around his hips, bury my hands in his hair, and kiss him like there's no tomorrow.

He starts walking through the kitchen to the living room, where he sits on the couch with me straddling his lap. Then, his hands start to roam.

"You didn't have to do that," I say when I come up for air. "It was a lot."

"They called you a liar." It's a simple statement. As if it's a no-brainer that he would do whatever needed to be done to defend me.

And it only makes me hotter.

"Thank you." I kiss him, lighter this time. "Thank you so much."

"You're welcome." His hands glide up and down the globes of my ass. Just a few days ago, I would have felt self-conscious with him, but he's seen me naked so much over the past four days, there is no reason to be shy. Not at all. He's seen it all, and he *likes* it.

I cross my arms over my lower stomach and pull my shirt up over my head, tossing it onto the floor.

Zane's pupils dilate as he takes in my breasts, covered by a soft pink bra today.

"I don't want to go slow," I inform him, and his eyes find mine. "I just want you, Zane."

He growls and stands, hurrying to the bedroom. We make quick work of stripping each other out of our clothes. My hands can't push his off fast enough. Finally, he reaches for the condom and plunges inside of me.

We moan in delight, and he starts to move, but it's not fast enough.

It's just not *enough*.

"Me." I push on his shoulder so he rolls over, and I can ride him, moving fast, grinding in the perfect way to push on just the right spot. I start to see stars. Zane grabs my ass and sits up, capturing my mouth with his, and I just explode, clinging to him as I rock and push against him.

"Jesus Christ," he mutters between clenched teeth as he follows me over.

We're tangled, chests heaving, and when our gazes lock, we start to laugh.

"I'm coming to school every damn day," he says. "If it gets this kind of reaction out of you."

"You were hot today," I inform him.

"I didn't even wear my uniform."

I laugh as I disentangle us and sit on the bed next to him. "Not Captain America. Zane Cooper. *You* were hot today. You made my kids happy, and you were generous and fun. And kind to Timmy, even though that kid is a challenge."

"I suspect he'll be less of one for a while," he replies and drags his hand down my hair. "I had fun, too. And I liked seeing you in your element. You're good with them, Aub. They respect you already. I know you were frustrated on Friday, but I think it's going to be a good year."

"Yeah, today was much better, even before you arrived. The beginning of the year is always a challenge as we all settle into a groove together. But I admit, this helped a lot."

"I tried to come toward the end of the day so no one would be expected to concentrate on actual schoolwork after I left."

"It was perfect timing," I agree. "The bell rang about fifteen minutes after you made your getaway."

"Good." He drags his fingertip down my arm, and the doorbell rings. "That's dinner."

He stands and pulls on his jeans—no underwear—and doesn't bother to button them up. He doesn't even pull on a shirt.

I reach for my robe and follow him into the living room, just as Amy walks inside, practically drooling over Zane.

I mean, who can blame her?

"Well, hello there. I hope I didn't interrupt anything."

"You didn't," I inform her, catching her attention. "We were finished."

Her mouth opens and closes like a fish, and then she blinks and looks down at the bag in her hands. "Oh, well. Good. Anyway, here's dinner. Baked salmon with asparagus and a side salad. You can just put it in the oven until you're ready for it."

"Thank you." I smile at her and take the bag from her. "We appreciate it. Have a wonderful evening."

"You, too." She looks from me to Zane and then shakes her head and leaves.

"What kind of weird woman shit just happened?" Zane wonders as he follows me into the kitchen.

"Okay, you're going to think this is ridiculous."

"Most likely, yes. But that's okay because I want to know."

I pull down two dinner plates. "I'm hungry. You?"

He nods, and I get to work plating our dinners.

"She's hot for you. And, let's be honest, I can't blame her. You're incredibly attractive, Zane. And you answered the door like that."

I point to him, and he looks down at himself and then back at me. "I'm covered."

I snort and then cough. "Sure, your *dick* is covered. But you didn't even put a shirt on. Come on, Zane. You even have that V thing in the hips, designed to lower a woman's IQ by at least seventy-five points. All I'm saying is, Amy wants you. Has no problem flirting with you. And would tumble into bed with you in a heartbeat. So, I was just—"

"Marking your territory?" he finishes for me.

I frown.

Do I have the right to do that?

I mean, we're sleeping together, literally. *And* we're having sex. A *lot* of sex.

But maybe he doesn't mean for this to be exclusive.

"Whoa, your brain just went into overdrive." He grabs the plate and sets it down, then takes my shoulders in his hands. "I see it, Aubrey. I understand."

"Maybe this isn't exclusive, and I put my foot in my mouth," I blurt out in complete mortification.

"Are you planning to fuck someone else?"

I blink rapidly and look up into his intense blue eyes. "Uh, no. I didn't plan to fuck *you*. But I like it. I like *you*. And I just assumed that if we're having sex, we're not having sex with anyone else. As long as we're having sex with each other. I'm babbling."

He laughs and kisses my forehead. "I followed. And I agree. I'm too busy thinking about getting you naked as often as possible to be distracted by anyone else, honey. You don't have to worry about that."

"Well, maybe in the future, you can wear a shirt when you answer the door?"

He grins. "I don't think that's too much to ask. And maybe you wear more than that skimpy little robe."

I glance down and notice that the robe has opened enough to show some cleavage.

"It got the job done, but I don't plan a repeat performance."

He smacks my ass lightly. "Okay then. I'm hungry."

"Let's eat."

* * * *

Oh, God, why did I come here?

I was just getting settled into this crazy little life with Zane, and now I'm at a girls'-night-out party with Natalie Williams and all of her friends.

There must be twenty-five women here.

Gorgeous women.

The gene pool in this room is so impressive, I don't even know what to say.

Like Zane, I don't know what happens at this kind of thing. I've never been invited to one. I pictured five or six women sitting around with drinks, trying on makeup with a dozen cupcakes sitting nearby.

This is not that.

Not even a little.

Luke and Natalie's house is…huge. With gorgeous water views, the place is something you'd see in a magazine. A wall of windows has been opened like an accordion so there's indoor and outdoor seating.

And if you choose outdoor, there's a pool.

The massive kitchen is covered in food, and the promised cupcakes are topped with pink frosting and little decals that have Amelia's logo on them. There's a separate bar area where a beautiful redhead shakes a shaker and fills pretty glasses with lemon wedges on the rim.

Amelia herself, whom I recognize from her YouTube tutorials, is organizing brushes and copious amounts of makeup on the dining room table that, by my calculations, comfortably seats twelve.

I do not belong here.

Going out for dinner is one thing, but this? This is another thing entirely.

Just as I'm about to text Zane and tell him to turn around and come back for me, Natalie rushes over and takes my hand.

"Oh, I'm so glad you came."

"Really?"

She laughs and leads me into the room. "Yes, absolutely. We went a little overboard, but this is a celebration, so I'm not sorry. Now, for some introductions. I don't expect you to remember everyone's names."

But I will. I'm used to remembering a school full of kids' names.

"Hi, I'm Meg," a pretty woman says. "We're a lot to handle, but we're a lot of fun."

I meet Jules, Samantha, Brynna, and Stacy, who are all in the kitchen, hovering over the food.

Amelia, and her sister, Anastasia, greet me at the dining table and then lead me outside to meet a dozen more women.

Once we've fully made the rounds, Natalie gestures and says, "That's all of us. Again, I don't expect you to remember. Just ask, or say, 'Hey you.'"

"I'll remember," I assure her.

"Okay, pop quiz," Lexi says. "Who am I?"

"You're Lexi." I start to point and rattle off the names. "Nic, Maeve, Izzy, Maggie. Meredith, Alecia, Joy."

I move around the room and correctly list everyone's names.

"I'm a teacher, you guys. Names are my superpower."

"Wow," Natalie breathes.

"Even I don't remember everyone's names all of the time, and I'm related to these people," Jules says with a laugh. "Here, you earned this."

She passes me a plate and leads me to the buffet table. To my utter shock, I'm simply brought into the fold as if I've been here forever.

As if they've been my friends since childhood.

The food is ridiculously good, and the company even better. When Maeve offers me a lemon drop, she sits right next to me, and we chat for about thirty minutes.

"Okay, Aubrey," Amelia says, crooking her finger at me. "Your turn, girl. Let's do a little makeover."

"Oh." I wave her off and shake my head. "That's not necessary. I love your products, and I'm happy to buy them."

"You might as well let her play," Nic says with a laugh. "This is what she lives for."

"You have such great skin," Amelia says as I sit in her chair, and she pushes my hair away from my face. "I'd kill for your cheekbones."

"Oh, please."

I know that I'm deficient in the looks department. I can't hold a candle to the other women in this room. I have a crooked nose, and there's just nothing special about the way I look.

It's okay.

"Honey, it's true," Amelia says softly. "Your skin is the bomb. What products do you use?"

"Soap and water?"

She pauses, staring at me for half a second. "That's it?"

"And a little moisturizer."

"Okay, now I hate you. Do you know how many women would *kill* for skin like this? Can I recommend some things?"

"Are you kidding? Of course."

Amelia Montgomery, makeup mogul, is giving me advice on my skin. Whose life is this?

"Okay, I want to stress sunscreen. I do see a little sun damage here."

"I grew up in Arizona."

"Ah, yes, that explains it. I have a great SPF that isn't oily. I'll give you some." She goes into detail about serums and moisturizers, and I must get glassy-eyed because she laughs and pats my shoulder. "I know, it's a lot."

"It sounds expensive," I admit.

"I know. It is. So, you can minimize it to three things. A good cleanser, a serum, and some moisturizer. And because you're so young, you probably don't need the serum yet, but you can't start too early."

"I like the minimal idea," I confess. "I'd just get confused if I had a seven-step regimen."

She laughs, and for the next thirty minutes, I sit still while she concentrates on my makeup.

Am I going to look like a drag queen when she's done?

I hope not.

"Oh, do the gold," Jules says when Amelia stares at her palate for a long minute. "With those amazing eyes, it'll be perfect."

"I think you're right," Amelia says with a nod. Before long, a small group stands around us, eating cupcakes and watching.

I've never been the center of attention like this in my life.

"Oh, I never thought of doing the eyeliner like that," Nic says. "I like it."

"Okay, we're finished," Amelia says after applying one last coat of mascara. She passes me the mirror, and I stare, transfixed.

"I still look like me."

"Of course, you do," Amelia says. "It's you, enhanced."

My eyes look a little bigger, and the eyeshadow is subtle. I felt her use all kinds of things on my face, but I can't tell. I just look a little more angular. You can't even tell that my nose is super crooked.

"You have great lips," Natalie says and takes a bite of cupcake. "You look fabulous. Here, give me your phone."

I pass it to her, and she snaps a picture of me, taps the screen a few times, and then hands it back.

"I just sent that to Zane. He'll swallow his tongue."

Before I can tuck my phone away, it rings.

"It's Zane." Everyone laughs around me as I answer and put him on speaker. "Hey there."

"I'm coming back to get you."

"What? Why? I'm not ready to go home."

"You're fucking gorgeous," he says, his voice intense. "I want to see you."

"Too bad," Jules says. "She's ours. You can have her later. It'll be good for you to pine after her a little."

"Sorry, I have to stay for a bit longer," I tell him but feel all warm and glowy inside, knowing that he's hot after me right now. It's even better knowing that he's attracted to me without all of the makeup. "But I'll make it up to you."

"Hell yes, girl," Maggie says with a wink. "Make it up to him."

I laugh and accept another lemon drop. "I'll see you soon."

I end the call and raise my glass. "To making hot men crazy."

"Amen," Brynna says, and we all drink. "Now, tell us about sex with Zane Cooper."

"And use all the dirty words," Alecia adds.

"And don't forget to tell us about the orgasms," Natalie puts in.

Oh, yeah. I like these girls. I like them a lot.

Chapter Eight

~Zane~

"What do you want to do this weekend?" I ask her. Aubrey's lying in bed, reading something on her iPad. We've been doing this, living together, sleeping together, for two weeks.

And the more I'm with her, the more I can't see myself living without her.

"I thought we were going to have dinner with Sabrina and Ben?" she asks with a frown.

"We are, but that's tomorrow evening. What should we do tonight?"

She sits up and, with the sheet tucked under her arms, faces me. "Clearly, there's something *you* want to do."

I shrug. Yeah, I have a plan, but if she already has her heart set on something, I can reschedule.

I just want to surprise her.

"I was thinking about just staying in tonight," she admits. "It was another busy workweek, and I'm tired. Maybe we could watch a movie or something."

She's on the right track with the movie idea.

"Will you let me surprise you with something?"

She raises an eyebrow. "Will I have to pack a bag? Put on workout clothes? Or do anything that requires brain function?"

I laugh and lean in to kiss her nose. "No to all of the above."

"Okay, then. Yes, you can surprise me."

I tug the sheet down and cup her breast. I never seem to tire of her. I can't get enough.

"Is this part of the surprise?"

"No, this is a bonus."

* * * *

"What should I wear?" she asks. She's wrapped in a towel, her hair and makeup done. Ever since she had her night out with Natalie and the others, she's worn makeup the way Anastasia showed her to.

I think she looks just as great without it, but this seems to give her more confidence.

"We're going casual this evening," I reply and gesture at my jeans and T-shirt.

"Okay, good." She disappears back into the closet. Less than five minutes later, she reemerges wearing jeans and a green sweater that makes her eyes look golden.

"You look amazing."

Her face lights up the way it always does when I compliment her, and I take her hand, leading her out to my car.

"Okay, tell me where we're going."

"No."

She frowns as she fastens her seatbelt and then props her fist on the opposite hand. "Best two out of three."

I raise a brow. "What are we playing for?"

"Whether you'll tell me where we're going."

I laugh, shake my head, and start the car. "Absolutely not. Besides, it won't take long to get there."

She sighs, links her fingers with mine, and sits back in the leather seat. My GPS leads me to the right place, just ten minutes from the condo.

I park, walk around the car to open the passenger door for Aubrey, and escort her to the theater.

"We're going to see a movie?"

I grin down at her and lean in to talk to the woman at the ticket counter.

"We're ready for you," she says with a wink. "Right this way."

"You didn't pay," Aubrey says, and we follow the young woman into the lobby.

"You'll be in theater one, just around the corner."

"Thank you."

"No one else is here," Aubrey whispers to me, looking around the empty lobby. "It's creepy."

"I rented it out," I inform her.

"All six screens?" she asks with wide eyes.

"Yeah. I wanted the place to ourselves. Now, do you want popcorn?"

"What kind of a question is that?" But before I can lead her to the concessions counter, she pulls me down for a kiss. "Thank you."

"We haven't even seen the movie yet."

"It's already the best date I've ever been on."

It's these little moments, the sweet things she says, that soften my heart. She's genuinely grateful. I've never seen her scoff.

And she has a heart of gold.

"Same here, sweetheart. Now, do you want butter on your popcorn?"

"Of course. And I want Milk Duds. And a Coke. When it comes to the movies, I'm a six-year-old."

I laugh and nod at the young man behind the counter. "Me, too. I want a large popcorn and a water."

"No sugar?" she asks.

"I'll eat one of your Milk Duds."

"No." She shakes her head matter-of-factly. "No, you won't. I don't share the duds."

I grin and then point at the M&Ms. "Better include those, then."

With loaded down arms, we walk into the empty theater and choose seats in the dead-center of the room.

"It's so quiet," she says with a smile. "And so weird."

"But fun weird, right?"

"Definitely fun," she agrees and shoves some popcorn into her mouth.

A man pops his head around the wall that leads to the lobby. "Are you ready, sir?"

"We're ready. Thank you."

"It's our pleasure. Enjoy."

"Wow," she breathes. "This is really fancy."

The lights go down, and the movie starts. My favorite film of all time. To Kill a Mockingbird.

"Oh my gosh." She gasps and smiles up at me. "Okay, this is extra fun. It's your favorite, and you brought me to the theater to see it."

There's that delight again, the kind that makes me feel like puffing up my chest.

"Here's hoping you don't hate it," I say and take the kernel of popcorn she offers me.

* * * *

"You rented out the *entire* theater?" Rina asks. "Like, the whole thing?"

"The whole thing," Aubrey confirms. We're having dinner the following night with my best friend and her husband.

"And what did you think of the movie?" Ben asks and passes a platter of steamed broccoli.

"It's so good. And so…" She pauses and slips a bite of chicken into her pouty mouth. "Good," she says again.

"Have you ever seen it in the theater before this?" Rina asks me.

"No," I reply. "And it was like seeing it again for the first time. So well done."

"It sounds like you two are having fun together," Rina says. "Zane tells me you're a teacher?"

"First grade," Aubrey confirms. "And Zane told *me* that you run a pantry? I'd love to help with that. Volunteer."

"I'd love the help," Rina says with a smile. "I'm running low on supplies again, but I have some things coming in soon. I'll need help with organization."

"I'm your girl," Aubrey replies.

"I could really use an introduction to someone at your school," Rina continues. "I've tried to get in there in the past, but I'm always shut down."

"What? Why?" I scowl at her. "Shouldn't they take the help gratefully?"

"Some schools claim they have it under control on their own," Rina says with a shrug. "I'm not always welcomed with open arms."

"I can introduce you to the principal," Aubrey says. "I know there are kids who could use your help. A full third of my students showed up without any of the supplies on the list that went out to their parents. Thank goodness I stocked up on things before the first day of school."

"Wait, you bought the supplies out of your own pocket?" Ben asks.

"Of course. Not all the kids have parents who can afford the supplies. Honestly, some don't care at all. There are others who buy more than needed to help ease the burden, but I usually end up buying enough for about eight students and then replenishing throughout the year."

"It happens so often," Rina agrees. "And how many of those kids are hungry when they arrive at school or don't have dinner? Too many. It's my mission to feed them, even if it's one at a time."

"I want to be you when I grow up," Aubrey says with a happy sigh and makes Rina blush.

I don't think I've ever seen my best friend blush.

"Okay, enough of that," Rina says, waving Aubrey off. "How about some dessert? I have strawberry shortcake."

"I'll help," I offer and pick up some empty plates to take into the kitchen.

We're far enough away from the dining room and Ben and Aubrey that when we get to the sink, Rina rounds on me.

"I like her," she says. "I like her *a lot*. And I see the way you look at her."

"How do I look at her?"

"Like you can't live without her." She grins. "Like you think she's the best thing since sliced bread."

"She's great," I agree with a nod. "Everything you heard at the table? That's her. What you see is what you get with her. She's *nice*. And I don't think she gives two shits about the career or the celebrity. Or even the money."

"Have you asked her?" Rina prods.

"No. It's not like it comes up in conversation. '*Do you have a problem with the fact that I'm rich and famous?*' That's stupid."

"It's not stupid. You've had too many women sleep with you because you *are* those things, Zane."

"Yeah, well, I know she's not doing that. Sometimes, I think she's with me *in spite of* it. And that's damn hot, too."

"For sure." She pulls the dessert out of the fridge. "So, you're sleeping with her."

"Yeah, it's been a few weeks now, I guess." I'm not going to tell Rina that Aubrey was a virgin. That's none of her business. "We spend pretty much all of our time together when we aren't working."

"And you're not getting on each other's nerves yet?"

"Not yet." I laugh and set sponge cake on little dessert plates. "I don't think there's much she could do at this point to irritate me."

I tell her about Aubrey's reaction to the chef flirting with me, and Rina laughs her ass off.

"Oh, I *really* like her. Good for her for standing her ground. You can be intimidating, Zane, because of who you are. And the fact that she's not afraid to be herself is refreshing."

"Oh, yeah. She calls me out on my shit," I confirm. "And I love that, too."

I clear my throat and sigh. Rina scowls at me.

"What? What's wrong? You don't like strawberries?"

"I love strawberries." I shift on my feet. "I don't know. I guess a tiny piece of me wonders if it's all too good to be true."

Rina shakes her head.

"It's not something I think of often because all I can think about is *her*, but now that we're listing all of the wonderful things she has to offer, I can't help but wonder—" I take a deep breath and rub my hand over my mouth. "Maybe she's a good actress, and I see what she wants me to see."

"You're a damn idiot."

I turn to see a fuming Aubrey standing behind me.

Chapter Nine

~Aubrey~

"I wonder what's taking them so long," I say and look over to the kitchen where Zane and Rina are chatting and plating the dessert. "I'll go see if they need help."

I walk up behind Zane, just in time to hear, "It's not something I think of often because all I can think about is *her*, but now that we're listing all of the wonderful things she has to offer, I can't help but wonder—" He takes a deep breath and continues softly. "Maybe she's a good actress, and I see what she wants me to see."

I open and close my mouth, registering hurt, anger, and complete incredulity.

"You're an idiot." It's the only thing I can think to say. Zane whips around, and his expression falls.

"Aub, I didn't—"

"You said it, didn't you? You know, you've said several times over the past few weeks: *I love how honest you are.* So, which is it, Zane? Am I honest, or am I a gold-digging actress?"

"You *are* an idiot," Sabrina agrees and shakes her head. "And you always sabotage good things."

"Just listen to me," he says, but I shake my head and turn to leave the room. I'm *pissed.* If he's had doubts about me, why didn't he just say something? Why not just ask?

"Thank you for a lovely dinner," I say to Rina and Ben, clenching my hands so they can't see them tremble with my anger. "I enjoyed meeting you both. Rina, I really do want to volunteer with you, so let's stay in touch, okay?"

"Of course," Rina says with a smile and then scowls at Zane.

"I'd like to go home now," I say politely. I will *not* have a fight in front of these nice people. I hate it when people have dramatic scenes in public.

"Aubrey," Zane says, but I shake my head and narrow my eyes at him. "Fine. Okay, I'll take you home."

"Thank you."

At the door, Rina pulls me in for a hug. "He's a moron, but he's not all bad. When you calm down a bit, listen to him, okay?"

I will *not* cry. "Thank you," is all I say, and then I walk to the car. I sit in the passenger seat and wait as Zane appears to get an earful from both Rina and Ben.

How could he say that? That maybe I'm just a good actress, and I've been playing him all this time? I tried to get him to move *out* when I saw that there was a mix-up with the condo for God's sake. *And* I was a virgin.

I wouldn't know how to play a guy if I had a handbook and a YouTube tutorial for reference. Especially not someone like Zane Cooper.

Zane finally joins me in the car, starts the engine, and pulls away from Ben and Rina's house, headed toward our condo. We live only about a three-minute drive away.

"Aubrey, I'm sorry."

"You know, that was a shitty thing to say," I reply immediately and point my finger at him. "I'm *not* the type of person who plays those kinds of games."

"I know." He sighs and pulls his hand down his face. "I don't even know why I said it. I *know* it's not true."

"It was hurtful. And if you said it, then a piece of you believes it. And, frankly, there's nothing I can do about that because I haven't done anything to you to make you think I'm interested in anything but *you*. I don't care that you're famous, Zane."

"Are you sure?" He pulls into his parking space and cuts the engine, then turns to me. "Are you sure that you *don't care*?"

I roll my eyes, get out of the car, and hurry up the stairs to the condo. I don't huff and puff like I did when we first moved in. Instead, I push inside, drop my bag on the kitchen island, and pace the room in agitation.

"What do you want me to say?" I demand. "That I'm starstruck every time I look at you? That it's a huge stroke to my ego that I lost my virginity to the likes of *Zane Cooper,* the most famous man in the world?"

"Some would," he replies with a shrug. "And have. Well, not the virginity part, but you know what I mean."

"No. I don't know what you mean, Zane. Because you don't *talk* to me about that stuff. I don't even know why you're hiding out here, in a tiny condo in Seattle. But you know what? It's none of my business." I hold up a hand when he looks as if he might start talking, then walk to the fridge and grab a bottle of wine and a glass. I stomp back to my bedroom. I don't slam the door because I'm not a child.

But I *really* want to.

I set my stuff down, lock the door, and sit on the edge of the bed. My heart hurts. My stomach is in knots.

And I'm so mad at him, I could throw something at his perfect head.

I hear him try to turn the doorknob and clench my eyes closed. I feel the tears now. My throat burns and feels tight.

"Open up, Aubrey."

I shake my head, even though he can't see me.

"Come on. I'm an idiot. Just open up, and we'll talk about this."

I don't want to. Maybe I'm being childish, but damn it, he hurt my feelings and embarrassed me in front of people who are important to him.

I don't want to talk to him. I don't want him to see me cry.

"I need some time alone," I say quietly, and he stops trying to turn the knob.

I hear him walk away, and I bury my face in a pillow.

All I can smell is *him.*

"Damn it," I mutter and set the pillow aside. I stare at the wine but decide against it.

I have to work tomorrow. No one likes to work with a hangover, especially when it's with small children.

Instead, I just roll into a ball on the bed and let myself have a cry-fest.

I've gotten good at keeping a hard shell over the years. Being the homely kid means getting teased a lot.

I have thick skin.

But I'd let myself soften toward Zane over the past few weeks. To trust that *he* wouldn't be one of the people who'd hurt my feelings.

And yet, here we are.

My feelings are hurt, my confidence is gone, and I'm just...sad.

* * * *

I left the condo before the sun came up this morning so I didn't have to see Zane.

Is that chickenshit of me? Yes. But I don't care.

It was a brutal morning. Mondays can be tough, because the kids are used to being home and in a different routine for a couple of days. So, there was some whining. Some yawning.

And, I admit, I was with them on both fronts.

I had a meeting this afternoon, so I had a sub come in for just a couple of hours to keep an eye on things until I return. I'm glad the school day is almost over, but I'm not looking forward to going home. I *know* I have to talk to Zane, but I'm putting it off.

Maybe I can come up with a few errands to run this afternoon before I go home.

"You really are chickenshit," I mutter to myself as I turn toward my classroom. I open the door, surprised that it's dead quiet, and all of the students are sitting at their desks, in rows, waiting expectantly.

"This is like something out of a creepy movie," I say and look toward Kelsey, my sub. "Everything okay?"

"Sure." She nods to the back of the room, and I follow her gaze, then feel my heart stutter.

There, in the back, sitting at a tiny desk, is Zane. God, he looks gorgeous in his blue button-down. It makes his eyes look even bluer—if that's possible.

I narrow my eyes, but before I can say anything, the children in the front row each hold up a white piece of poster board with black writing.

PLEASE JUST TALK TO ME.

I read the words and then look back at him, shaking my head as if to say, "*Really?*"

The second row picks up their signs.

HE'S REALLY SORRY, MISS S.

"That's not fair, Zane," I whisper. I have to swallow hard, so I don't cry.

I prop my hands on my hips as the third row lifts their signs.

LIFE'S NOT FAIR SOMETIMES.

I feel my jaw drop. Kelsey gasps behind me.

"How did you know I'd say that?"

It's the fourth row's turn now.

BECAUSE I LOVE YOU.

More tears fill my eyes, and I shake my head slowly. Zane's face registers panic, and then he races to my side and wraps his arms around me.

"Shh, don't cry. Shit, don't cry, Aubrey."

"He said the s-word," I hear Timmy say with a giggle.

I sniffle, and Kelsey steps over to us and says quietly, "I'll stay through the last hour. You go, Aubrey."

"Are you sure?"

"Absolutely." She winks and passes me my purse. "Have a good evening."

Zane holds my hand, and we silently make our way out to his car. I swipe at the tears on my cheeks, relieved when I get in the vehicle so no one but he can see me cry.

The drive home is even quiet.

When we get up to the condo, Zane takes my hands and kisses them both.

"I'm so sorry," he says at last. "Honest, I'm so very sorry. I know you're mad and that what I said was shitty, but I need you to hear me out before you decide that you don't want to have anything to do with me."

I frown and then bark out a laugh. "I'm not *that* dramatic, Zane. I'm pissed at you, but I'm not kicking you to the curb. Yet."

"Really? Oh." His tired face relaxes just a bit. "I can say with certainty that before last night, it never even occurred to me to suggest that you might not have been truthful over the past few weeks. I never got that vibe from you at all."

"Then why did you *say* it?" I demand and pull my hands away so I can pace. I always pace when I'm worked up. "You embarrassed me, Zane. More than you hurt my feelings."

"Rina and I were talking about you. About how great you are. She really likes you. And I was telling her about some of the fun things we've done. And then my stupid imagination started to run away from me a bit. I might have some baggage in this department." His shoulders slump. "Come on, let's sit."

"I do better on my feet."

"And I want to sit with you. I gave you your way last night." He catches my hand in his and pulls me to the couch. "You asked about why I'm here. I hadn't dated in a while, and then I met a woman through work. Not an actress. She's in costuming. Anyway, I asked her out and started dating her. Slept with her *one time*. She called the media and told them we were in a committed relationship. Which is annoying but wouldn't be a big deal. I figured I'd release a statement and deny and then move on with my life."

He takes a long, deep breath, pushes his hands through his hair, and then keeps going.

"But she threatened to accuse me of rape if I didn't pay her."

"What the hell?" I demand, immediately full of rage. "Who is this bitch? I'll kick her ass. Why do people suck? Why do people pull this kind of shit?"

"That was all my first reaction, too." He sighs and then shrugs. "She seemed pretty normal and down to earth when I met her. Turned out to be unhinged. I have a team of lawyers on it, and I know that nothing will come of it in the long run. But I don't have the cleanest reputation thanks to my misspent youth, and Hugh thought it would be best if I just got away for a while until the whole thing blew over. I didn't do anything wrong, so I'm not hiding. I'm just out of LA while it's handled."

"You could have just told me that."

"There was no need to bring it up. And then I was too preoccupied with *you* to give it much thought."

"I'm not an actress," I say flatly. "I wouldn't know how to play with a man's head, let alone manipulate and try to ruin them. I don't have time for it. It wouldn't even cross my mind."

"I know." His voice is soft. "I *know*. And I'm sorry for being a douche last night."

"I guess you'll have moments of douchiness if this thing between us lasts a while."

"I plan on it lasting a *very* long while," he replies. "I know that I'm only supposed to be in Seattle for a limited time, but there's no reason I can't move here permanently. I can commute to LA when I need to. I can work more with Luke. And, hell, I can do whatever the hell I want."

"I. You. I'm sorry, what?"

He smiles and leans over to kiss me softly. "I told you earlier. I love you."

"No, the *kids* held up a sign that said it."

His expression sobers, and he drags his fingers down my cheek. "I love you, Aubrey Stansfield. I fell hard and fast, and I don't plan on that ever changing. You've made me a better person."

"You've given me so much," I whisper and cover his hand with mine. "Confidence, affection, laughter. You've changed me."

"That makes two of us."

"I love you, too," I say at last. "And we'll figure the rest out."

Epilogue

~Aubrey~
Ten Months Later

I sit and stare at our Christmas tree, full of gratitude and love for the life Zane and I have built together in Seattle over the past year. It wasn't always easy. True to his word, he sold his house in Beverly Hills and bought a beautiful home that overlooks the water. We've been roommates since the day we met.

It's unbelievable when I think about it too hard.

We spent last night with Rina and Ben at their place, exchanging gifts and eating Chinese food—which is Rina and Zane's tradition for Christmas Eve.

And now, Christmas morning, I woke early and came out into our open living room to turn on the lights and enjoy them as the sun came up.

It's rainy outside, but I can see the mist hovering over the water of the Sound. My coffee is fresh.

And the man of my dreams is snoring in our bed.

Life just doesn't get much better than this.

Last night, Rina asked me how I'm adjusting to this new lifestyle, and the answer was easy.

"Zane and I love each other. His career can be a challenge, but we don't sweat the small stuff. As long as we communicate, understand each other, and have trust, everything else is small stuff."

"Why are you up?"

I turn and smile at my sleepy man as he pads into the living room and sits next to me, taking my mug and a drink.

"I don't know. I just woke up. But I wanted to let you sleep. I like the tree."

"I'm glad. It was the biggest one on the lot, and you just had to have it."

"We have tall ceilings," I remind him. "A short tree wouldn't look right."

"If you say so." He kisses my cheek. "Everything okay?"

"I'd say everything's pretty much perfect. How are you?"

"I'm excited to give you your presents."

I scowl at him. "You gave me like twelve things last night."

"That was Christmas Eve."

"Zane, I don't need a bunch of stuff. I have everything a person could want. You donated so much money to my school, they don't even know what to do with it all."

"Oh, they know what to do," he says with a grin. "They're going to fund all of the lunches and make sure no kid goes hungry. They're also going to make sure all of the kids have the supplies they need. Teachers shouldn't have to pay for that out of pocket."

Is it any wonder I'm completely in love with him?

"You've done enough."

"Well, there might be a couple more things." He smiles innocently.

"You first." I jump up, grab the shallow, square box wrapped in red and gold from under the tree, and present it to him. "This is for you."

He takes it, shakes it, smells it.

"It's not food."

"You never know. I love cake."

I shake my head with good humor while he unties the bow, then works on the paper. Inside is a movie script. It's yellowed, and the edges are a little crinkled.

But when Zane reads the first page, his eyes find mine in surprise.

"Aubrey."

I smile softly. "Luke helped me get it. It was Gregory Peck's script from *To Kill a Mockingbird*."

"I don't know what to say." He gently opens the pages and reads the handwritten notes in the margin. "This is priceless. My God, Aubrey, how did you find it?"

"I have to have some secrets." I wrinkle my nose. "You have literally *everything* in the known universe. You're not the easiest man to buy gifts for, so I'm keeping my secrets close."

He kisses me, long and slow, then cuddles me close.

"I could go for some coffee," he says.

"Me, too." I press my fist to the flat of my opposite hand. "Best two out of three?"

"You're on." He mirrors my stands, and I smile.

"Okay, go."

I land on scissors, he on rock.

I narrow my eyes. "Again."

This time I'm paper, and he sticks with rock. His smile is smug.

"One more time," he says.

I end up on rock, and he switches to paper, winning this round.

"Okay, I have to go pour us coffee," I say and start to get up, but he pulls me back down.

"That's not what we were playing for," he says.

"No?" I cock a brow. "Just what did you win, Mr. Cooper?"

He holds up his hand, and between his thumb and forefinger is a diamond ring the size of a baby's fist.

"You have to marry me," he says and watches me with bright blue eyes. "You have to make me the luckiest man in the world and marry me."

"Oh." I bite my lip and feel my heart fill to bursting with love for this man. "I think we both win in this scenario."

That grin flashes, and he slips the ring onto my finger.

"Is that a yes?"

"I don't have a choice. You won."

"That's right." He tugs me against him and holds on tight. "I won."

* * * *

Also from 1001 Dark Nights and Kristen Proby, discover Shine With Me, Wonder With Me, Soaring With Fallon, Tempting Brooke, No Reservations, Easy With You, and Easy For Keeps.

Sign up for the 1001 Dark Nights Newsletter
and be entered to win a Tiffany Key necklace.

There's a contest every month!

Go to www.1001DarkNights.com to subscribe.

**As a bonus, all subscribers can download
FIVE FREE exclusive books!**

Discover 1001 Dark Nights Collection Eight

DRAGON REVEALED by Donna Grant
A Dragon Kings Novella

CAPTURED IN INK by Carrie Ann Ryan
A Montgomery Ink: Boulder Novella

SECURING JANE by Susan Stoker
A SEAL of Protection: Legacy Series Novella

WILD WIND by Kristen Ashley
A Chaos Novella

DARE TO TEASE by Carly Phillips
A Dare Nation Novella

VAMPIRE by Rebecca Zanetti
A Dark Protectors/Rebels Novella

MAFIA KING by Rachel Van Dyken
A Mafia Royals Novella

THE GRAVEDIGGER'S SON by Darynda Jones
A Charley Davidson Novella

FINALE by Skye Warren
A North Security Novella

MEMORIES OF YOU by J. Kenner
A Stark Securities Novella

SLAYED BY DARKNESS by Alexandra Ivy
A Guardians of Eternity Novella

TREASURED by Lexi Blake
A Masters and Mercenaries Novella

THE DAREDEVIL by Dylan Allen
A Rivers Wilde Novella

BOND OF DESTINY by Larissa Ione
A Demonica Novella

THE CLOSE-UP by Kennedy Ryan
A Hollywood Renaissance Novella

MORE THAN POSSESS YOU by Shayla Black
A More Than Words Novella

HAUNTED HOUSE by Heather Graham
A Krewe of Hunters Novella

MAN FOR ME by Laurelin Paige
A Man In Charge Novella

THE RHYTHM METHOD by Kylie Scott
A Stage Dive Novella

JONAH BENNETT by Tijan
A Bennett Mafia Novella

CHANGE WITH ME by Kristen Proby
A With Me In Seattle Novella

THE DARKEST DESTINY by Gena Showalter
A Lords of the Underworld Novella

Also from Blue Box Press

THE LAST TIARA by M.J. Rose

THE CROWN OF GILDED BONES by Jennifer L. Armentrout
A Blood and Ash Novel

THE MISSING SISTER by Lucinda Riley

THE END OF FOREVER by Steve Berry and M.J. Rose
A Cassiopeia Vitt Adventure

THE STEAL by C. W. Gortner and M.J. Rose

CHASING SERENITY by Kristen Ashley
A River Rain Novel

A SHADOW IN THE EMBER by Jennifer L. Armentrout
A Flesh and Fire Novel

Discover More Kristen Proby

Shine With Me: A With Me In Seattle Novella

Sabrina Harrison *hates* being famous. She walked away from show business, from the flashing bulbs and prying eyes years ago, and is happy in her rural Oregon home, dedicating her life to her non-profit.

Until Hollywood calls, offering her the role of a lifetime. In more than ten years, she's never felt the pull to return to the business that shunned her, but this role is everything Sabrina's ever longed for.

Now she has to get in shape for it.

Benjamin Demarco's gym, Sound Fitness, continues making a name for itself in Seattle. And now, he finds himself with the task of training Sabrina, getting her in shape for the role of her life. He's trained hundreds of women. This is his job. So why does he suddenly see Sabrina as more than just another client? His hands linger on her skin, his breath catches when she's near.

He knows better. Soon, she'll be gone, living her life. A life that doesn't include him.

* * * *

Wonder With Me: With Me In Seattle Novella

Reed Taylor doesn't pay much attention to the holidays—until he receives a surprise present. Four-year-old Piper is the daughter he never knew about, and with the death of her mother, is also now the roommate he never expected. He's determined to make their first Christmas together one she'll never forget.

Noel Thompson has gotten her share of strange requests in her career as an interior designer. The call to design a beautiful home for Christmas is more like a dream come true. And that was *before* she met her new employer—sexy and mysterious, he's everything she ever hoped Santa would bring her.

As Noel showers his home with holiday spirit, Reed showers Piper with love. And the busy life he's created for himself no longer seems nearly as important as the one Noel is helping him build with his daughter. But if he can't convince his decorator to stay, this could be the only year he feels the true wonder of the season.

* * * *

Tempting Brooke: A Big Sky Novella

Brooke's Blooms has taken Cunningham Falls by surprise. The beautiful, innovative flower shop is trendy, with not only gorgeous flower arrangements, but also fun gifts for any occasion. This store is Brooke Henderson's deepest joy, and it means everything to her, which shows in how completely she and her little shop have been embraced by the small community of Cunningham Falls.

So, when her landlord dies and Brody Chabot saunters through her door, announcing that the building has been sold, and will soon be demolished, Brooke knows that she's in for the fight of her life. But she hasn't gotten this far by sitting back and quietly doing what she's told. *Hustle* is Brooke's middle name, and she has no intention of losing this fight, no matter how tempting Brody's smile -- and body -- is.

* * * *

No Reservations: A Fusion Novella

Chase MacKenzie is *not* the man for Maura Jenkins. A self-proclaimed life-long bachelor, and unapologetic about his distaste for monogamy, a woman would have to be a masochist to want to fall into Chase's bed.

And Maura is no masochist.

Chase has one strict rule: no strings attached. Which is fine with Maura because she doesn't even really *like* Chase. He's arrogant, cocky, and let's not forget bossy. But when he aims that crooked grin at her, she goes weak in the knees. Not that she has any intentions of falling for his charms.

Definitely not.

Well, maybe just once…

* * * *

Easy For Keeps: A Boudreaux Novella

Adam Spencer loves women. All women. Every shape and size, regardless of hair or eye color, religion or race, he simply enjoys them all. Meeting more than his fair share as the manager and head bartender of The Odyssey, a hot spot in the heart of New Orleans' French Quarter, Adam's comfortable with his lifestyle, and sees no reason to change it. A wife and kids, plus the white picket fence are not in the cards for this confirmed bachelor. Until a beautiful woman, and her sweet princess, literally knock him on his ass.

Sarah Cox has just moved to New Orleans, having accepted a position as a social worker specializing in at-risk women and children. It's a demanding, sometimes dangerous job, but Sarah is no shy wallflower. She can handle just about anything that comes at her, even the attentions of one sexy Adam Spencer. Just because he's charmed her daughter, making her think of magical kingdoms with happily ever after, doesn't mean that Sarah believes in fairy tales. But the more time she spends with the enchanting man, the more he begins to sway her into believing in forever.

Even so, when Sarah's job becomes more dangerous than any of them bargained for, will she be ripped from Adam's life forever?

* * * *

Easy With You: A With You In Seattle Novella

Nothing has ever come easy for Lila Bailey. She's fought for every good thing in her life during every day of her thirty-one years. Aside from that one night with an impossible to deny stranger a year ago, Lila is the epitome of responsible.

Steadfast. Strong.

She's pulled herself out of the train wreck of her childhood, proud to be a professor at Tulane University and laying down roots in a city she's grown to love. But when some of her female students are viciously murdered, Lila's shaken to the core and unsure of whom she can trust in New Orleans. When the police detective assigned to the murder case comes to investigate, she's even more surprised to find herself staring into the eyes of the man that made her toes curl last year.

In an attempt to move on from the tragic loss of his wife, Asher Smith moved his daughter and himself to a new city, ready for a fresh start. A damn fine police lieutenant, but new to the New Orleans force, Asher has a lot to prove to his colleagues and himself.

With a murderer terrorizing the Tulane University campus, Asher finds himself toe-to-toe with the one woman that haunts his dreams. His hands, his lips, his body know her as intimately as he's ever known anyone. As he learns her mind and heart as well, Asher wants nothing more than to keep her safe, in his bed, and in his and his daughter's lives for the long haul.

But when Lila becomes the target, can Asher save her in time, or will he lose another woman he loves?

* * * *

Soaring with Fallon: A Big Sky Novel

Fallon McCarthy has climbed the corporate ladder. She's had the office with the view, the staff, and the plaque on her door. The unexpected loss of her grandmother taught her that there's more to life than meetings and conference calls, so she quit, and is happy to be a nomad, checking off items on her bucket list as she takes jobs teaching yoga in each place she lands in. She's happy being free, and has no interest in being tied down.

When Noah King gets the call that an eagle has been injured, he's not expecting to find a beautiful stranger standing vigil when he arrives. Rehabilitating birds of prey is Noah's passion, it's what he lives for, and he doesn't have time for a nosy woman who's suddenly taken an interest in Spread Your Wings sanctuary.

But Fallon's gentle nature, and the way she makes him laugh, and *feel* again draws him in. When it comes time for Fallon to move on, will Noah's love be enough for her to stay, or will he have to find the strength to let her fly?

Shine With Me

A With Me In Seattle Novella
By Kristen Proby

Sabrina Harrison *hates* being famous. She walked away from show business, from the flashing bulbs and prying eyes years ago, and is happy in her rural Oregon home, dedicating her life to her non-profit.

Until Hollywood calls, offering her the role of a lifetime. In more than ten years, she's never felt the pull to return to the business that shunned her, but this role is everything Sabrina's ever longed for.

Now she has to get in shape for it.

Benjamin Demarco's gym, Sound Fitness, continues making a name for itself in Seattle. And now, he finds himself with the task of training Sabrina, getting her in shape for the role of her life. He's trained hundreds of women. This is his job. So why does he suddenly see Sabrina as more than just another client? His hands linger on her skin, his breath catches when she's near.

He knows better. Soon, she'll be gone, living her life. A life that doesn't include him.

* * * *

It's Monday morning, and I've been awake for an hour. I'm on my second cup of coffee and just bit into my bagel when the doorbell rings.

He's prompt, I'll give him that.

All I know is that my new trainer's name is Ben. That's it. This should be interesting.

I open the door and am immediately under intense male scrutiny—which I expect from a trainer.

He's going to be getting me into shape.

What I don't expect are the long silence and the gaping mouth.

"Hi, I'm Ben."

I shut the door in his face and turn away, dialing Luke's number as I walk across the room.

I hear the door open behind me, but I don't turn around. I pace and mumble, waiting for Luke to answer.

Sure, gawk at the washed-up movie star, you jerk.

"Hello?" Luke says.

"Seriously, Luke?"

Suddenly, the phone is taken out of my hand, and Ben ends the call, earning a glare from me.

"I wasn't staring because you're a movie star. I was staring because I wasn't expecting you to be quite *this* gorgeous."

I prop my hands on my hips. Seems I might be speechless now, and that doesn't happen often.

"I'm Ben," he repeats.

"Sabrina."

He looks me up and down again as my phone rings in his hand. To my surprise, he answers.

"Hey Luke, Ben here. She's fine." He passes me the phone with a smirk on his cocky lips, and I press it to my ear.

"Hi."

"Everything okay there?"

"Yeah, false alarm, I guess."

"Okay, let me know if you need anything. Have a good day."

He hangs up, and I slip my phone into my pocket, then turn and lead Ben to the kitchen. Mostly, I have to look away from him so I don't make a fool of myself. Because the man is hot with a capital *H*.

About Kristen Proby

New York Times and USA Today bestselling author Kristen Proby has published more than sixty romance novels. She is best known for her self-published With Me In Seattle and Boudreaux series. Kristen lives in Montana with her husband, two cats, and a spoiled dog.

Discover 1001 Dark Nights

On Behalf of 1001 Dark Nights,

Liz Berry, M.J. Rose, and Jillian Stein would like to thank ~

Steve Berry
Doug Scofield
Benjamin Stein
Kim Guidroz
Social Butterfly PR
Ashley Wells
Asha Hossain
Chris Graham
Chelle Olson
Kasi Alexander
Jessica Johns
Dylan Stockton
Kate Boggs
Richard Blake
and Simon Lipskar

Made in the USA
Las Vegas, NV
06 November 2021